"I would always hesitate to recommend as a life's companion a young lady with quite such a vivid shade of red hair. Red hair, sir, in my opinion, is dangerous."

Jeeves by P.G. Wodehouse

Relic
by
Kate Fitzroy

©KateFitzroy2020

Prologue

'I've always believed that business should never be mixed with pleasure but...' Henry stroked my shoulder as he spoke, then sighed and left his sentence unfinished.

He had no need to say more as there was still at least an hour before family breakfast. As we moved closer together in the creaky four-poster bed, I closed my eyes and thought of everything but business. Pleasure, yes, such pleasure... we were nearly late for breakfast.

My father looked up over his Sunday Times as we came into the breakfast room and smiled benignly,

'Good Morning, lovebirds, how very punctual you are. There's coffee already brewed and waiting on the sideboard. Help yourselves. Allie, dear, why don't you give your brother a shout?'

I shook my head,'No, Pa, it's Sunday, for Goodness sakes… Suzie and Sam are up at the crack of dawn every other day of the week. Let them sleep on and...'

Before I could finish my sentence, the breakfast room door flew open and my brother, Sam, entered in running shorts and a vest. He came over to me and said,

'Ah, how sweet of you, Sis, or did you just want to eat all the croissants before I had a chance. You've always been a greedy little red-headed piggy.'

'Don't come near me. You're disgusting. Go and have a shower and come back down. Do I have to remind you over and over that my hair is auburn and not red? Get away from me.'

Sam jogged up and down in front of me, pretending to throw small punches in my direction and suddenly I felt a sisterly rush of affection and said,

'You're mad. Why on earth would anyone want to go for a run in this icy weather?'

'But it's fantastic out there. There's a sharp frost and Suffolk is at its very best. Suzie ran with me... she loved it.' Sam swiped two croissants from the warming tray and laughed down at me. Henry moved forward and held out an empty bread basket,

'Here, Sam, take the basket.' Sam suddenly looked abashed and said,

'Oh God, Henry, you and your Eton manners. You are much too civilised. Thanks. I'll go and have a shower now.'

'Good idea.' Henry said in a quiet voice and I stood back, admiring the little scene as my brother stood eye to eye with my lover. They were of exactly the same height and probably weight, but Henry was as dark as Sam was fair. They held their gaze for a brief moment and then Sam spun on his heel and ran out of the room.

I sighed, 'I suppose they were the last two croissants. I bet Sam and Suzie already had one breakfast before they went for a run.'

Henry turned to me and smiled and, as usual, my knees turned soft and trembly. He had a variety of smiles and the best teeth I had ever seen, including in toothpaste advertisements. Now his smile was just slightly mocking but full of love. He reached across the sideboard and took a white napkin off another basket.

'Ecco! A basket of brioches, croissants and your favourite almond ones. Your mother certainly knows how to keep her family happy. Help yourself.' He gave a little bow and clicked his heels together as I selected the biggest almond croissant. Then he added, 'Your hair is most definitely the most beautiful auburn, but Sam is right about one thing, you are a dreadful Princess Piggy.'

My father put down his newspaper and laughed, 'Quite right, Henry, Allie has always had a huge appetite. I've never understood how she eats so much as there's nothing of her. Always a skinny little thing.'

'When you have quite finished talking about me,' I said, moving to sit beside my father at the table, 'Would you pour me some coffee?'

'Certainly, my dear, but it's quite true, you know, you do eat enormous amounts of food for your size.'

'I just have a very good appetite...' I replied, sipping my hot coffee, '...for food and all the good things in life.'

'That's true.' Henry said as he sat opposite me at the table. I didn't dare catch his eye as I knew exactly what he was thinking, but then he added, 'I mean, your love of fine art, especially.'

My father nodded, 'Yes, she always loved beautiful things... and horses, of course.'

'Is this going to be a long discussion of my character or can we move on?' I said, 'Perhaps we should discuss this idea you have, Pa, of sending us into the depths of Norfolk tomorrow?'

'Well, it would do me a great favour if you could go over to Farley Hall and just take a look at their Constable. Old Sir Peregrine is in dire straits and has to sell something to pay for the repair of the roof. Allie, Do you remember Sir Peregrine ?'

'Vaguely. I remember a tennis party there one summer ages ago. My schoolfriend, Fenella, invited me. It's a huge pile, isn't it? I think it was dilapidated then and the court was covered in moss... the whole day was rather like a scene from P.G. Wodehouse. I don't remember Mr Jerome much except he was extraordinarily tall and kept saying 'what's that!' ... I had no idea anyone actually said it.'

'That's Sir Peregrine, rather a relic of the past, but Sir Jerome, to you, my dear. Don't forget when you meet him. That is, if you are kind enough to go over there.'

Henry poured me another coffee and said,

'Of course, we'll go. I'd love to go up to the Norfolk coast and I've checked on the map. Farley Hall is not more than an hour from Newmarket and if it is a genuine Constable... well, it would be rather exciting. We can mix business with pleasure, I'm sure.'

As Henry spoke, Rosso, his dog, a huge Scottish wolfhound, slipped quietly into the room and settled under the table with his long head on my foot. I reached down and stroked him. The dog yawned and then sighed heavily.

'I know, Rosso, I know.' I said quietly, 'A hunting we shall go again.'

Chapter 1

"I always advise people never to give advice."
                                P.G. Wodehouse

Later that day, after a long ride out in the Suffolk countryside, I was sitting by the fire and toasting my toes and a crumpet on a long fork. My father had asked Henry to help him move two of the horses from the stable yard and my brother was still out riding with Suzie. My mother was sitting on the sofa behind me and as I twiddled the crumpet around, browning it nicely, I realised I had been set up for a heart to heart.

'It's so lovely to have you here for the weekend, dear.' My mother said quietly, flicking the pages of Vogue and trying to sound casual.

'It's lovely to be here, Ma, as usual.' I neatly prodded the crumpet onto a plate and handed it to my mother. 'Here, you have the first one and while you butter it, why don't you ask me whatever it is you want to know?'

'What do you mean, Alicia?' My mother's voice was mild but she usually called me Alicia when she was either worried or cross with me. I often thought it was a strange name to be landed with... not quite Alice, which I should have preferred. Most people called me Allie and my brother often called me Al or Als. Now, Henry's mother, the aristocratic Contessa Claudia di Palliano, had dubbed me Alessandra. It was as though my name had a life of its own. I sighed, thinking how lucky Sam was to have such a simple name and then I speared another crumpet and held it close to the blue flames leaping from the side of one of the huge logs in the grate. I really didn't mind what anyone called me, I decided. In fact, there wasn't anything that I minded at all at the moment. I was so happily in love with Henry that the whole world seemed perfect. I sighed again and my mother said,

'You do seem very happy and content, dear, so much more relaxed lately.'

'Yes, Ma, I'm sure you've noticed that I am head over heels in love with Henry. It does make for a sweet life.'

'I'm so glad, Alicia. Henry seems to be a fine young man. Your father and I are very fond of him already but we can't help being just a tidgy bit worried. Not trying to advise you, of course but, well, yes we are a little concerned.'

Here we go, I thought to myself, and twiddled the crumpet round and round, rather too near the flame.

'Worried?' I said, 'About me? There's absolutely no need, Ma.'

'Are you sure you should have left your marvellous job at the auction house... such good prospects? We met your ex-boss at a charity ball last week and he still wants you back. I didn't know quite what to say. He seemed to think that working for the Palliano's was... well, rather risky.'

'Risky?' I turned to look at my mother and the crumpet dropped into the centre of the fire. 'Why on earth would he say that? The Palliano antique business was founded ages ago and is flourishing.'

My mother was silent for a moment and the air was filled with the not unpleasant aroma of burning crumpet. Then she said,

'I'm sure you're right. Rupert Edmonton is such a diehard Englishman. Maybe it's just because the Henry's family is Italian.'

I laughed and speared anther crumpet and replied,

'Probably and a certain amount of jealousy that they should be so successful. Anyway, Henry never wanted to be an antique dealer, he studied art and was just beginning to exhibit his watercolours when his stepfather, Gold, died and Henry had to step into the breach, sort of thing.'

'Hmm, yes, indeed.' my mother's voice was dangerously casual, 'Very good of him, of course. His mother does seem to be a very demanding woman, charming, absolutely charming but…' Her voice tailed away into another silence and I continued to twirl the crumpet around. My mother was right, the Contessa was possibly the most imperious and autocratic woman I had ever encountered, but there was no also no doubt that I had become very fond of her. I was about to say so but my mother stood up and came over to the fire and said,

'And then, there's the Contessa's new man, Federico Maneri. I gather they're engaged to be married. It will be her third husband and…'

'And he's hideously wealthy and you're worried he's some sort of Mafiosi godfather?' I laughed and dropped another crumpet into the flames.

'I think you'd better give me the toasting fork, dear.' My mother said calmly, ' You're just not concentrating.'

'Well, I'm beginning to feel like I'm being grilled myself. Really, Ma, you have absolutely nothing to worry about.'

I passed the toasting fork to my mother and stood up and stretched. I kissed my mother lightly on her pink cheek and then threw myself down on the sofa, quite sure that I was right.

Chapter 2

"The voice of Love seemed to call to me, but it was a wrong number."
P.G.Wodehouse

My mother and father waved us off the next morning, standing side by side with their arms linked. I caught a fleeting glimpse of them in the driving mirror and then as I drove around the bend in the drive, they were lost to sight. Much as I loved them, I was glad to be alone with Henry and in the comfortable and familiar surroundings of his old Alfa Romeo.

'That was a lovely Sunday, Allie, your parents are so very kind. It seems dreadful to say that I am glad to be leaving and alone again with you.'

As so often seemed to happen, Henry had voiced my own thoughts and I was about to tell him so when Rosso stood up on the back seat and pushed his long nose forward between the front seats. Henry laughed,

'Sorry, Rosso, of course, I'm glad to be with you, too. Now don't go into your jealous dog act, please.'

Rosso rested his paw on my shoulder, delicately licked my ear and ignored Henry.

'Come on, Rosso, I was just saying...' Henry began and then gave up as Rosso turned around and settled down on the back seat and put his paws over his ears.

'You've done it now, Henry.' I said, unable to resist smirking, 'It will be ages before Rosso forgives you.'

'I know, I know. All I meant was...'

'I think you should give up. You'll only make matters worse.' I settled into the driving seat and glanced in the mirror to see that Rosso was now feigning sleep. I'd been travelling long enough with Henry and Rosso to know how they liked to play games. Henry said,

'I do believe my dog prefers you to me nowadays. What sort of canine fidelity is that? Why should I be the one in the doghouse?'

'No idea.' I said, shortly and then added, 'It was a lovely Sunday, wasn't it, but Ma took the opportunity of a heart to heart when you escaped to the stables with Pa.'

'Really? In that case, we were both set up. As soon as your father and I were out of the house, he talked to me about horses and my polo-playing and then, suddenly, he practically asked me what were my intentions.'

'Your intentions? Sounds like something out of a Jane Austen novel. Whatever do he mean?'

'Well,' Henry drawled the word as though giving himself time to think, 'Well, after a load of questions about my career, financial status and general morals... I think the gist of it was that if I ever harmed you in any way at all, emotionally or physically, then he and Sam would break every bone in my body.'

I burst out laughing, 'Really? Oh well, if that's all then...'

'All? He seemed deadly serious.'

'Oh, I expect he was and he's probably talked with Sam, too. But don't worry they...'

'Of course, I'm not worried. I would never harm an auburn hair on your pretty head and I intend to devote the rest of my life to making you happy but...'

'So, that's all right then, isn't it? Anyway, I was on the other end of all that with Ma worrying that your Italian family were a bit dodgy... and about your Ma's new flame, Federico Maneri. It's all ridiculous, let's forget it.'

'Dodgy? The Palliano's? I rather wish we were. No, we're just the fag-end of a long line of aristocrats scraping a living.'

'Hmm, well, scraping isn't quite how I'd describe it. You are mega-successful, in fact.'

'We get by, I suppose, but long gone is the Castello di Palliano near Frascati.'

Henry sighed and I glanced quickly sideways at him and said,

'Do you miss your family home? How old were you when you left it?'

'Good Lord, no, I don't miss a thing. I was only a kid of seven or so when my father died. My mother decided that we should travel and off we went around the world. I have no idea how or why she sold up everything. Maybe she had to... I have no idea.'

'So, you ended up in London?'

'Yes, eventually I was packed off to school and Mamma took the house in Chelsea.'

I nodded and tried to imagine how Henry had survived such an unstable childhood. My own life had been so very traditional and orderly and, most of all, loving. I was quiet for a moment and the Alfa slid effortlessly along on its silent electric engine, while Rosso gently snored, now genuinely asleep, on the back seat. Henry broke the silence and said,

'I've always been happy enough but now that I have met you, I know true happiness. I love you, Allie. When we've checked out this Constable, I thought we could carry on up to the coast. I googled for a hotel and there looks like a comfortable one in a place called Burnham Market.'

'Hmm, that sounds a lovely idea. But Burnham Market is full of Londoners. I know a lovely pub in Thornham, right on the sea. We could try there.' I leaned against Henry and thought how lovely it would be to go straight there.

Henry raised his hand and gently stroked my hair away from my face. I sighed and Rosso stirred and yawned.

Chapter 3

"The fascination of shooting as a sport depends almost wholly on whether you are at the right or wrong end of the gun."
P.G.Wodehouse

Henry had been quite right, in under an hour the sat-nav informed us we had arrived at our destination. The only problem was that there wasn't a house in sight, let alone the grand stately pile that I vaguely remembered. I slowed down and pulled into a muddy lay-by and looked at Henry.

'I think the sat-nav has lost the plot.' I said, stretching my arms above my head and peering through the windscreen and up at the pale blue Norfolk sky. The bare branches of the trees on either side of the narrow lane arched over us, frosted white and still. Rosso pushed his head between us and licked his lips and sighed heavily, then turned back and curled up on the back seat again.

'Not our fault we seem to be lost, Rosso.' Henry said, 'And it's no help sulking. Do you want to come with me and take a look around?'

'Not really,' I replied although I knew that Henry had been talking to Rosso. 'It's icy cold out there and what is there is see?'

Henry buttoned up his jacket and said,

'Well, we can't just sit here. I'll take a look around. I expect the sat-nav has given up because Farley Hall is surrounded by private land so they couldn't map it.

Don't you remember the place at all, Allie? I thought you said you had played tennis here... that your schoolfriend lived here?'

'Hmm, well, yes, but it was ages ago. I must have been about fifteen and I was just dropped off as far as I remember. No idea.'

Henry sighed and said, 'Right, you two remain here and be useless. Strange that whenever I don't want you to come with me you always stick to me like glue. Now, you...'

'Rosso and I only come with you when we think you're about to be foolhardy.'

'Foolhardy?'

'You know, when you get one of your sudden ideas that invariably end up in trouble if not downright danger. I mean, there's nothing dangerous around here so...'

I stopped speaking abruptly as there was the sudden crack of a rifle shot and the small birds that had been huddled together in the frozen branches rose in the air and flew in circles over the car.

'Dear God! Was that a gunshot?' I said, holding my hands over my ears.

Before Henry could answer there was another crack and the sound of a bullet winging through the hedge very near... too near... to where I had parked.

Henry leaned over me, pressed the electric starter button and sounded the horn. I had always thought that one of the best things about Henry's veteran Alfa was the low, imperious sound of the hooter. Now, as Henry pressed it another three or four times it seemed to fill the icy air with its important sound. Rosso suddenly stood up and growled as the bushes on Henry's side parted and a very red face under a tweed hat glared at us.

Henry wound down his window and said calmly,

'Good day! Do you by any chance know Farley Manor?'

The air from the open window made me shiver and I pulled my scarf closer around my neck as more of the red-faced man slowly emerged from the hawthorn hedge. Now, I could see he was carrying a rifle and a bag of game. He was extraordinarily tall and by the time he had clambered over the ditch, I had recognised him as Sir Peregrine Jerome, the father of Fenella, my schoolfriend. His hair curling out from under his hat was greyer and his face more lined, but I remembered the piercing blue eyes and protruding teeth. Yes, definitely Sir Peregrine. I was about to introduce myself but at that moment he stumbled and fell back into the ditch. Henry jumped out of the car, took charge of the rifle and then offered a hand to Sir Peregrine who was floundering amongst the brambles and frozen ditch water.

'God dammit!' I heard Sir Peregrine say and then closed my ears to the string of oaths that followed. Henry seemed to be having some difficulty heaving at Sir Peregrine and just as he made some progress, two black labradors arrived on the scene and jumped into the ditch and on top of Sir Peregrine. Rosso leapt past me and out of the passenger door and threw himself happily into the fray. There was a lot of barking from all three dogs, although they seemed to be enjoying themselves as Sir Peregrine continued to flail around and swear heartily. Deciding that this was probably not the best time to introduce myself, I leaned across the passenger seat and closed the door. There didn't seem any point in us all freezing.

Chapter 4

"She looked away. Her attitude seemed to suggest that she had finished with him, and would be obliged if somebody would come and sweep him up."
   P.G.Wodehouse

'You'll stay the night, of course.' Sir Peregrine was standing with his back to the roaring fire and steam was rising from his tweed breeches in a pale cloud. 'Won't hear of anything else. What's that, Girlie?'

He turned to his wife, a tiny anxious woman, who now stood wringing her hands and looking up at Henry and then to me. Her whole appearance seemed to proclaim that she wanted nothing to do with anything, especially anything that her husband had arranged.

'This is Agatha, what's that? Yes, the wife, don't you know..'

Sir Peregrine had briefly introduced us when we had finally arrived at Farley Hall in general disarray. Sir Peregrine limping and leaning heavily on Henry, Rosso bounding around with the two labradors and showing off dreadfully and me, trying to remind Lady Agatha that we had met before. She had fluttered around us trying to understand quite who we were and how we had saved Sir Peregrine from a ditch and barely disguising the fact that she would rather retire and read a book. The fact that Sir Peregrine had nearly shot us dead had not been mentioned. Now, grouped around the stately fireplace I began to thaw out and managed to say,

'It's lovely to be here again,' I was lying, of course, as the vast room was only slightly warmer than outside and there was an icy blast of wind strong enough to lift the tattered curtains away from the huge windows... but I continued firmly,

'I don't suppose you remember me, I'm Alicia Ponsonby.... I was at school with your daughter, Fenella.'

'Fenella?' Lady Agatha looked vaguely around as though expecting one of the portraits hanging on the walls to give her a clue. For a brief moment, I thought that somehow I was wrong, that I had never played tennis here or been their daughter's schoolfriend for five or six years. I blinked and was about to try again when Lady Agatha suddenly focussed on me and said,

'Why, of course, my dear, of course, I remember you now. Your beautiful auburn hair, yes, yes and you played so very well. Yes, you and Fenella quite won the day.'

I sighed with relief and Henry said quickly, as though trying to profit from a moment of sanity,

'Alicia's father suggested we should come over and see you... something about a Constable?'

Sir Peregrine who had been shaking out his breeches and shedding a good amount of wet earth and twigs on the flagstone floor turned around with his back to us and shouted,

'What's that? Good God, what a coincidence to meet you in the back lane. Amazing. That's life, isn't it?'

There didn't seem to be a sensible reply to make to this, so I remained silent, but Henry tried again,

'Alicia is the expert in fine art and I'm...'

Sir Peregrine spun around, nearly falling over and Henry reached out and steadied him, saying,

'Careful, sir. You took quite a fall just now, maybe you should sit down.'

'Sit down? No, no, no... a hot bath and glass or two of whisky is what I need. You two get settled in and I'll be back down for luncheon. Make yourselves at home, do. What's that? Ponsonby's girl, eh?' He turned his surprisingly piercing blue-eyed gaze on me and added, 'What a beauty, you are, m'dear. Pleasure to have you stay with us, yes, yes.' He straightened up to his full, impressive height and towered over his wife as he said, 'The blue room, don't you think, Girlie? What's that? They should be comfortable there.'

He then limped and tottered from the room, zig-zagging between sagging sofas and delicate what-nots of fine china, his labradors at his heels. We were all silent, watching his exit, waiting for him to collide or crash but he made it to the door and without turning around raised a hand in farewell and shouted,

'Back in no time, starving hungry already. Order the vittles, Girlie, and get Benson to bring up something or other from the cellar, something good. Toodleloo.'

We remained in silence for another moment and I'm sure that Henry was sharing my thoughts. There was absolutely no way we would be staying the night at Farley Hall.

Chapter 5

"He had just about enough intelligence to open his mouth when he wanted to eat, but certainly no more."
                                        P.G.Wodehouse

'More pud, anyone?' Sir Peregrine clapped his hands loudly and looked around at us hopefully. 'I shall anyway. Nothing as good as Nanny's recipe for bread and butter pud. It's the raisins that make it. What's that?'

Benson, an elderly thin man in a shiny dark suit, hovered behind Sir Peregrine, holding aloft a burnt Pyrex dish with the remains of the pudding. I spoke hastily,

'No, thank you so much, but no more for me.'

I held my hand over my plate to stop any more food being dished to me. Rosso, his head conveniently resting on my knee under the table, had already helped me out with most of the meal. The food was truly awful and I didn't dare even look at Henry... well, not since I had managed to swap his empty plate of beef stew for my full one earlier in the meal.

Sir Peregrine, his protruding yellow teeth pointed in my direction and his beady blue eyes concentrated on me alarmingly, said,

'Can't I tempt you, little Ponsonby? There's nothing of you, no flesh on your bones. You need fattening up a bit. What's that? Have some more pud?'

I looked up entreatingly at Benson and he gave a discreet nod and moved back a pace. Fortunately, Sir Peregrine gave up on me and turned to Henry,

'How about you, young man? I suppose you only go for Eye-tie nosh... all that pasta baloney? What's that?'

We had been long enough at the meal for us both to realise there was no need to answer any of Sir Peregrine's questions. He blundered on and on and, if it hadn't been for my father, I kept thinking, we should never have been here, Constable or not.

Henry had made several attempts to draw the conversation toward the painting but without any success. Agatha had possibly caught on to the idea that it was the reason we were visiting, but I couldn't be sure. When she wasn't anxiously trying to keep Sir Peregrine from drinking copious draughts of the very good Burgundy, she seemed to lapse into a beatific dream state. I really couldn't blame her and had felt myself drifting off into oblivion on several occasions. I sat up straight in my chair and decided it was time to put an end to the seemingly endless flow of Sir Peregrine's words. Unfortunately, in sitting up straight, I somehow managed to dislodge the back of my chair. Henry threw out his arm and just saved me from falling backwards as the legs of the chair splayed and parted company from the back.

I jumped to my feet and said,

'Oh, my goodness, I am so sorry.'

I looked down at the broken Chippendale fragments and Rosso, who had dodged out of the way, pushed his head up from under the tablecloth and looked at me mournfully.

Sir Peregrine roared with laughter and said,

'Good Lord, there goes another one. How many do we have left now, Girlie?' He turned to Agatha who just twisted her hands together and gave a little nod.

'I am so very sorry.' I repeated, 'Please allow me to have it mended.'

'Mended! What's that? Lord, no, don't bother, we have an attic full of broken chairs. If it couldn't stand the weight of a whippersnapper like you then it's not a chair but a few scraps of wood.'

I caught Henry's eye and I know we were both thinking that it was the most beautiful example of Chinese Chippendale and simply had to be professionally repaired. Perhaps we were both wondering, too, how many more there might be in the attic. Henry said,

'As I'm sure I mentioned earlier, Sir Peregrine, my family are in the antique business and it would be a pleasure to have it mended in our workshop in Mayfair.'

'Mayfair, eh, what's that? Ah, how I remember my mis-spent youth in the clubs around there... they were the times, such times.' Sir Peregrine nodded rather sadly and I was worried as his head sagged forward that he was about to fall asleep. But quite suddenly, his chin came up and he slammed his hand on the table, knocking over his glass of wine and roared,

'Just had an idea! What's that? Could I ask you to look at my Constable while you're here? Never sure if it's the quite the bees knees, don''t you know, what, but it's hung on the landing for as long as I can remember and always called 'The Constable.' I know it's an awful cheek to ask a guest a favour but...'

Henry stood up and said very quickly,

'My pleasure, sir, I'd love to see it but Alicia is the art expert.'

Sir Peregrine stood up and swayed alarmingly for a moment and looked at me, then said,

'What? Ponsonby's girl? What's that? Art expert, whatever next?'

Chapter 6

"I could see that, if not actually disgruntled, he was far from being gruntled."
P.G.Wodehouse

'We nearly made it!' Henry said, slapping his knee in exasperation. 'If only Benson hadn't asked whether he should park the Alfa.

We were sitting as close as we could to the smouldering log fire and drinking tea. I yawned,

'Well, you could hardly refuse to take Sir Peregrine for a little joy ride, I suppose. I just don't understand that he had no recall of being in it after you rescued him from the ditch.'

'Oh, I don't know. He'd had quite a shock, I think, and his ankle is very swollen. He was fascinated to find that the Alfa has an electric engine. He was actually very knowledgeable about engines. He quite came to life for a while. Ah well, I suppose it is best that he takes a rest.'

'Hmm, maybe.' I said doubtfully. I was never as sympathetic or tolerant as Henry. His brief moment of exasperation had already passed but I felt most disgruntled. 'I feel like we've been kidnapped. Benson has a lot to answer for in my opinion. Who asked him to take our bags to the Blue Room?'

'Yellow room, now, apparently. Lady Agatha told me quietly that the Blue Room was out of use due to weather damage.'

'Oh God, can't we just demand our bags and go?' I stood up and angrily poked one of the logs, causing a few sparks to fly up the ancestral chimney.

'We'll wait for another hour and see what happens. Lady Agatha said she'd be back from her meeting with the Women's Institute in the village then. We can't possibly leave without saying some sort of farewell. Anyway, your father has asked us a favour. I don't want to let him down.'

'I do!' I said, sitting down on Henry's lap, 'He must have known how doo-ally the Jeromes are and if they ever had a Constable they have probably lost it.'

'Not even the Jeromes could lose a Constable, surely?' Henry looked at me in alarm and I was sitting close enough to admire the way his dark eyebrows formed perfect arches. I kissed his forehead and said,

'I wish you were a dodgy sort of Italian Palliano like my parents suspect. Right now we could be snooping around the Hall finding all sorts of treasures. Chinese Chippendale chairs, Constables... all sorts of glorious relics.'

'Don't be ridiculous, my love. You know quite well we can't do any such thing. It would be incredibly bad manners.'

I sighed, 'I know, I know, but it would be fun. Perhaps we could bribe poor old Benson to show us around. He looks like he needs a new suit.'

'Even more ridiculous, my sweet love, Benson is definitely the loyal sort. Anyway, stop all your fancy ideas right now. I know you're just bored and you are always so badly behaved when you're bored. Have another cup of tea. It's rather fine, Fortnum's Royal blend, I think.'

'How on earth would you know that? Although, why do I ask? It's just the sort of ridiculous thing you would know. But don't think you can placate me with a cup of tea, Royal or otherwise. Anyway, it's probably frozen in the pot by now and as for the scones, just look at them. They're sort of grey.'

'Are you surprised after that lunch? Which reminds me, you swapped my empty plate with yours, didn't you? That frightful stew! You deserve to be thoroughly punished.'

'I thought you hadn't noticed, Henry dear!'

I jumped off Henry's lap and dodged away from him and ran across the room to the window. Henry followed in pursuit and Rosso looked up from where he was stretched out in front of the fireplace and joined in as we chased around the room. I dodged behind a large wing leather wing chair and was finally cornered. Henry held me tight in his arms and began to kiss me. Finally, feeling warmer than at any time since we had met Sir Peregrine in the ditch, I relaxed and reached up to run my fingers through Henry's liquorice dark hair. At that moment, the door creaked open and Benson entered, stopped in the doorway and began to turn around to discreetly leave. I wriggled free from Henry and said,

'Hello, it's Benson, isn't it? Thank you so much for the tea but we'd like you to show us to our room.'

Benson nodded and I thought I saw a shadow of reluctance or doubt cross his face. Henry said,

'We'd like to wash and brush up, if you'd be so kind as to show us to the Yellow Room or is it the Blue?'

Henry had that aristocratic, rather diffident way of asking a servant 'to be so kind', which I always found very amusing. It wasn't as if Benson had any choice in the matter and what would Henry have said if Benson refused 'to be so kind.' As it was, Benson looked even more doubtful as he said,

'Certainly, sir. I've turned on the heating in the Yellow Room but you may prefer to wait here beside the fire a little longer?'

'I see.' Henry nodded and we both returned to our chairs by the fire, followed closely by Rosso. 'Probably a good idea, Benson, thank you.'

'Would more tea be desirable, sir?' Benson began to take the tray of tea and grey scones away and I said quickly,

'Yes, please. I think it would be a very good idea.'

Benson gave a little bow of his silver-grey head and left. When the door had closed behind him, I added,

'I still feel like we've been somewhat captured. I'm going to kill my father for getting us into this.

Chapter 7

'In a series of events, all of which had been a bit thick, this, in his opinion, achieved the maximum of thickness.'

P.G.Wodehouse

The Yellow Room was even colder than I had thought any room could be. The heating turned out to be an ancient electric fire, large and dusty and giving out very little heat. Henry approached it and reached down to put his hand in front of the flickering false lumps of coal.

'I do believe it's just a light bulb, there doesn't seem to be any heat at all. Maybe it's on the wrong switch position?'

'I shouldn't touch it, Henry, please don't. It's bound to give you an electric shock.'

'I doubt there's enough power to do that.' Henry turned and looked at me, 'It is freezing in here, isn't it? Put my jacket on. I can't think why no-one has lit the fire.' He walked over to the empty grate and looked at it as he took off his jacket. 'Here, put this round you.'

I snuggled into Henry's rather nice cashmere jacket and enjoyed the remnant warmth from his body. There was his perfume, too. I pushed my nose into the lapel and breathed in the elusive aroma of Henry... something like all the wild herbs of Provence mixed with that first whiff of a sea breeze when you reach the coast.

'We could go to bed, I suppose.' I said doubtfully, looking at the small four-poster bed and the drooping yellow canopy.

'I never thought I'd say this, my love, but no... not a good idea. I'm not sure we wouldn't both die of hypothermia.'

'Gosh, you've never turned down the idea before. But you're right,' I patted the satin eiderdown and added, 'It's so cold it feels damp.'

'If the chairs weren't Hepplewhite I could smash them up and get a fire going but...' Henry picked up one of the delicate chairs and examined it closely, 'Hmm, really beautiful... just look at the inlaid bellflowers... satinwood and maple, I'd say.'

'Do you have to talk antiques right now, Henry? Rosso made the right decision to stay by the fire.'

Henry looked around hopelessly and then said, 'And you were right earlier, Allie, we can't stay here. Let's pack our bags and leave.'

'I thought you said it would be incredibly rude?'

'Well, frankly I don't think the Jeromes have been perfect hosts. It's a bit thick, isn't it? Peregrine's obviously sleeping off the effects of all the wine he downed at that dreadful luncheon and Girlie Agatha has disappeared off to the village. I mean, really, it's not on.'

'Good. I absolutely agree. And what's more, you're beginning to talk like Sir Peregrine… a bit thick? You'll be saying 'what ho' and 'what's that' soon and 'don't you know. Do you think it's like teenagers saying 'like' every other word?'

'If I can't talk about antiques then how can you talk semantics? And why are we both getting so bad-tempered? Is it the first symptom of frost bite?'

'Probably. Anyway, it's very difficult to be jolly when it's this cold.'

I went over to the tall wardrobe that stood between the two windows and cautiously opened it.

'Look, all our clothes are hanging up and our bags in the bottom of the wardrobe. Let's pack quickly and get out.'

Henry came over and pulled out our two bags, his large Louis Vuitton and my shabby backpack and opened them. I reached up and took the one posh dress that I had brought with me off the heavy wooden coat-hanger when, suddenly, there was a long and piercing scream. It seemed to come from outside our bedroom door, close by... possibly in the corridor... and then it was quickly repeated by another ghastly strangled howl of pain.

I hadn't thought it possible to feel colder but the dreadful cries made my blood freeze in my veins.'

Chapter 8

'Hell, it is well known, has no fury like a woman who wants her tea and can't get it.'
　　　　　　　　　　　　P.G.Wodehouse

Henry rushed out of the room and I followed, still clutching the wooden coat-hanger. The corridor was shadowy with just a little dark afternoon light filtering through a curtained window at the far end. There was nothing to be seen or heard. Henry had stopped still in the middle of the corridor and I stood close behind him and clutched his shirt. Neither of us said anything and my heart was beating fast, pounding and sounding loud in my ears. Henry moved forward slowly and I followed, reluctant to move but even more reluctant to let go of him.

'Anyone there?' Henry's voice broke the silence but his question dropped like lead into the cold air and remained unanswered. He moved forward again and so did I... now we were nearing the long window at the end of the corridor. I stifled a scream as one of the shabby brocade curtains moved slightly. Henry leapt forward so fast that I lost my grip of his shirt and stood petrified, watching as Henry reached the window and pulled the curtain aside. There was nothing to be seen and Henry turned to me,

'Just the draught from the window, the wind must have stirred the curtain.'

I still stood rooted to the spot and replied, hearing my own voice squeaky with fear, 'But the screams, the dreadful cries...'

Henry came back and put his arms around me and I felt faint with relief at the warm comfort of his body heat.

'How do you stay so warm?' I murmured, leaning into him.

'I've no idea, especially as you have my jacket. That murderous scream was enough to curdle my blood though... what the hell happened? Perhaps old Peregrine had a nightmare?'

'I thought Benson said we had this wing to ourselves?'

Henry shrugged, one of his rather fine broad-shouldered shrugs, and I snuggled into him.

'Let's go and pack. The whole place is too Gothic, it's like being in a horror movie... not to mention freezing cold. Whoever it was screaming has my sympathy but I do not want to know more.'

'I suppose so,' Henry said slowly and my heart sank as I realised he was feeling he should do something about it... find out who was screaming and why. It was my opinion that his education and elegant manners frequently led him into trouble.

'Henry, please, let's just go. There's still time to drive up to the coast and find a nice place to stay, preferably with central heating and a roaring log fire.'

I am sure that Henry was about to be persuaded but, just at that moment, Lady Agatha appeared at the other end of the corridor with Rosso and the two labradors at her heels.

'Ah, there you are!' She called out to us, her voice now not vague or hesitant but with a different sharp ring of aristocratic authority. 'Your wonderful dog led me to you. He seems to understand anything I say. Come along now, cocktails are being served in the library and our other guests have arrived. Do hurry up!'

Suddenly everything seemed terribly normal. Rosso stood wagging his tail happily and waiting for us as Lady Agatha turned on her ancient Timberland heel and went back to the staircase, followed by the romping labradors.

It just didn't seem possible to tell Lady Agatha that we had heard murderous screams. I slipped off Henry's jacket and gave it to him, then Rosso, as though unable to wait any longer, lolloped along the corridor and circled around us. We began to walk toward the stairs when Rosso suddenly whirled around and scampered back to the window and pushed his nose into the curtain. I grabbed Henry's hand, cold fear returning, as we both watched in fascination at Rosso whimpering and pawing at the tattered edge of the curtain.

Henry called to Rosso, his voice more commanding than usual and Rosso gave one last push with his nose into the curtain and then galloped back to join us as we made our way downstairs.

Chapter 9

"She looked as if she had been poured into her clothes and had forgotten to say when."
  P.G.Wodehouse

'Of course I remember you, Alicia. You were at school with Fenella. We came to several of your school plays and I particularly enjoyed your Puck.'

I could almost feel Henry trying not to laugh as the very large woman in front of us greeted me enthusiastically. Did I know her, should I remember her… it was certainly embarrassingly true that I had played the part of Puck in my school's dreadful rendition of Midsummer Night's Dream. I played for time and said,

'Goodness, how good to see you again.'

My reply ended rather abruptly as I couldn't add her name.

'You don't remember me do you? I'm Fenella's godmother, Rowena Hardcastle.'

She held out a plump be-ringed hand and I shook it, trying not to show my surprise. Rowena Hardcastle I did remember but the woman in front of me was at least four dress sizes larger than I remembered. I hastily turned to Henry and said,

'May I introduce you to Henry di Palliano. Henry, this is Lady Rowena Hardcastle…'

then, just in time, I remembered, '…
Charlotte's mother.'

    Henry did his usual Etonian v Italian thing of shaking her hand and giving a little bow of his head and click of his heels. Lady Rowena looked up at him and I could tell that I no longer existed. I sighed with relief as Henry made light conversation and enquired more about my role as Puck. The whole exchange had been made more difficult by the fact that I had still been holding the wooden coat-hanger in one hand behind my back. I took the opportunity of slipping it onto a chair near the wall before looking around at the other guests. Sir Peregrine was in full flow, holding a dominant position in a small circle of people gathered near the fire. His height and long outstretched arms made him a most prominent figure and his long grey hair curled wildly around his flushed face as he talked. To add to the effect, he was dressed extraordinarily in a red robe embroidered richly with what looked like dragons and flames. Was Sir Peregrine an old age hippie? I smiled at the thought as I heard the odd loud 'what's that' and 'what-ho' sprinkled in his speech. Somehow it just didn't work. I saw Lady Agatha by the window, brave woman to stand the icy draught, talking animatedly to a man almost as tall as Sir Peregrine but dressed very formally in a dark grey lounge suit and silk tie…

possibly an old school type? Then, before I could examine the other guests in more detail, although I did spot a dog collar on a plump short man listening to Sir Peregrine, my attention was drawn back to Lady Rowena as she said,

'And how are your parents?'

I hastily replied, as though I had been listening all the time,

'Very well indeed, thank you.'

Again, I knew I should say more but, for the life of me, I couldn't think what. Henry came to my rescue,

'Lady Rowena was telling me how very well you played the part of Puck even though you knocked Titania off her throne of flowers.

I glared at Henry as he smiled down at me and the full horror of my teenage embarrassment returned. Perhaps I had rather over-played my part, bouncing and leaping around the small stage in my green tights and tunic but, surely, Titania, a very plump girl, had fallen off her throne all by herself? Now Lady Rowena was chortling merrily, her treble chins wobbling and her hand resting on Henry's arm to support herself. Hmm, I thought, Titania might not be the only fatty to tumble. Fortunately, before I could sink any lower in unkind and pejorative thoughts, Lady Agatha announced that dinner was served.

Chapter 10

"Some minds are like soup in a poor restaurant - best left unstirred."
P.G. Wodehouse

Dinner was no improvement on lunch. In fact, it was probably worse as I was seated between the roly-poly vicar, 'call me Malcolm' and another male guest who drank whisky throughout the meal. When Benson had taken away my untouched bowl of watery soup, I had turned as etiquette demanded, to talk to him. It was not very successful as it was harder than talking to a bottle of whisky. I tried and failed to make any conversation and resorted to the usual comments on the English climate. This resulted in a sad nod of his head and his sombre one-word reply,'Indeed.' I sighed as this didn't offer much to go forward with so I gave up and tried not to look down at my plate of overcooked beef. Henry had been seated next to our hostess and I glanced sideways and was surprised to see him talking to Benson as his wine glass was refilled. There was something conspiratorial about the way Henry was talking into Benson's ear. What was Henry up to? Perhaps he was asking about the Constable? Surely we could give up on that now? When Benson reached me I covered my glass with my hand and he moved on. If Henry was drinking then I was determined to remain cold sober so that I could drive us away as soon as we could escape. It certainly wasn't difficult to remain cold. I began to slowly eat small morsels of my bread roll as I was actually starving but not hungry enough to face anything on my plate. I regretted not being able to wash the bread down with a gulp of red wine as I managed to catch Henry's voice complimenting Sir Peregrine on his claret.

'A stunning vintage, sir, I've only had the pleasure of drinking a 2015 Pomerol once before. So rich and velvety.'

Sir Peregrine was at the head of the long table and he raised his glass to Henry as his voice boomed out,

'Glad you like it, what, not sure who you are, but what does it matter?'

There was a lull in the conversation the length of the table and Lady Agatha seated at the foot of the table and on the other side of the roly-poly vicar, spoke sharply, 'Peregrine, you know quite well that young Henry is here with Alicia, Fenella's school friend. Surely you remember him pulling you out of a ditch this morning?'

At this there was some laughter of the horse-neighing type and Sir Peregrine joined in, out-neighing them all and said,

'Yes, yes, of course. You're the fellow with the emasculated Alfa Romeo Pininfarina.' He gave one more guffaw, his protruding teeth glinting in the candlelight, and added, 'Incredible coincidence to meet you, what's that?'

Surely, I thought this is Henry's opportunity to mention the Constable but no… he began a long explanation, sprinkled with 'sir' of the merit of the electric engine installed in the Alfa. I sighed and turned back to the roly-poly vicar and talked across him to Lady Agatha,

'Not such a coincidence, really, you see my father…'

The roly-poly vicar interrupted me and said,

'Am I right, is your father Edward Ponsonby, the horse trainer in Newmarket?'

I could hardly ignore him so I nodded and tried to continue,

'You see, Lady Agatha, we were on our way here…'

Again I was interrupted by the Reverend Roly-Poly,

'I follow the horses, don't you know, and your father is one of my favourite trainers.'

I stifled another sigh as I knew what was coming next. My father's reputation followed me around and I was always being asked for hot tips. I was surprised that a man of the cloth should be so interested and I looked at him more closely. His eyes behind his round wire spectacles were shining greedily and I had been around the racing world long enough to recognise a gambler when I met one. His next words confirmed my suspicions.

'Does your father have any particular hopes for the next flat season?'

I shook my head and said firmly,

'I have no idea at all.' This was not strictly true as my brother, Sam and I both held on to our interest in our father's stables but we had been brought up to be discreet. I added,

'I work in London, I'm a researcher for Palliano's antique business. I'm here with Henry di Palliano to examine…'

I faltered to a complete stop and Roly-Poly had lost all interest in me and was pushing a slab of overcooked beef into his mouth. Even Lady Agatha had turned to the man on her right, the tall man I had noticed before. I sat back in my seat, hoping not to break it, and completely gave up.

Chapter 11

"Everything in life that's any fun, as somebody wisely observed, is either immoral, illegal or fattening."
P.G.Wodehouse

'I can't believe you agreed to stay, Henry. How could you?' I was walking wearily up the huge staircase, tired, angry, cold and hungry. I turned to Henry who was following me and saw his eyes were riveted to the lower section of my back view. 'And don't think I'm going to get into that cold damp bed either. Apart from the fact that Peregrine's brother told me that the Yellow Room was in the haunted wing... honestly, Henry, what were you thinking?'

'I was thinking all sorts of things, my love. You must agree it is much too late to travel now. The roads will be icy and we'd never find a hotel open... we haven't booked anything. Anyway, here we are.'

We had arrived at the long corridor and I eyed the curtain at the far end suspiciously. There was no movement and for a moment I wished that Rosso was with us. As so often happened, Henry voiced my thought.

'Well, I can't believe that Rosso chose to sleep in the kitchen with his new Lab friends. What a deserting rat.'

'You can't call a dog a rat.' I said grumpily, 'And I wish I could sleep in the kitchen, too. I bet there's an enormous old Aga kicking out heat.'

Henry moved in front of me as we arrived at the Yellow Room door, opened it for me and then put his hand on my backside and gave me a little push. I gave a little jump into the room and then gasped in surprise. It was warm, so warm and redolent of the pine logs burning merrily in the hearth. There were candles and tea-lights on every flat surface, the bedside tables, the mantelpiece, the chest of drawers and the dressing table… all glimmered with soft light. It was like walking into a miracle.

I span around in the centre of the room and said, my voice piping in surprised delight,

'How did you do it?'

Henry came over to me and put his arms around me and kissed the top of my head,

'Well, I had to do something. I promised your father only earlier today that I was determined to make sure you are always happy.'

'My father already has a lot to answer for… goodness, was it only today... but I must say, this is a very good result. Never mind the Constable.'

'Ah, well, I do know a little more about the Constable but before I tell you all… you'd better have something to eat.'

'Eat?' I heard my own voice now squeaking as Henry pointed to a table by the fireside. I ran over to it and pulled aside the white napkin and discovered a pleasing pile of dainty sandwiches and a packet of Bourbon biscuits. I snatched up the top triangular sandwich and popped the whole thing in my mouth. Speaking with my mouthful, I said,

'Mmm, smoked salmon. So yummy!' Then I added reluctantly, 'I suppose you want one?'

Henry laughed and said, 'No, they're all for you. I ate dinner, unlike you, I'm not a food snob.'

'You so are… well, usually you are.' I took another sandwich and sat down in the wing chair by the fire munching happily and kicking off my shoes. Henry came over and sat in the wing chair opposite and gave me one of his toothpaste ad smiles, his white teeth gleaming in the firelight as he said,

'You forget I had survival training at Eton. I used to get so hungry I'd have eaten my desk. By the time I left it was improving but when I started there I was appalled.'

'Poor little Enrico, it must have been horrid. My brother always says the same about Westminster. He counted on my mother sending food parcels.'

'Lucky Sam, my mother was not the food parcel sending type. Very occasionally she would turn up and take me to Cliveden for luncheon. But not often.'

There was a wistful look in Henry's eyes and I felt my heart contract at the thought of the young Enrico being plummeted into life at Eton.

'It must have been awful. Were you very miserable?'

Henry looked at me in surprise and said, 'God no, I soon worked out the system. I had my Italian upbringing to rely on and, even at that age, I understood bribery and corruption. I soon had things sorted out.'

I laughed and said, 'And you're still sorting things out, aren't you? I bet you gave old Benson a huge wad of money to warm the room up.'

'Hmm, well, he forgot the flowers but, apart from that, I suppose he's done his best.'

'It's so warm in here now that flowers would wilt in no time. So you bribed and corrupted poor Benson?'

'Well, we came to an understanding. I had a quick word with him and then managed to slip away while everyone was drinking coffee and you were flirting with the chap in the lounge suit. I had a further little chat with Benson. That's when I found out about the Constable.'

'Really, what did he tell you?'

'Benson's not sure it's original but apparently it's listed in the archival inventory of the Manor. Date of purchase etcetera. It hangs in a corridor to the right of this wing.'

'Goodness, how amazing! I can't wait to see it.' I ate the last sandwich slowly, now feeling quite full and added, 'What do you mean, flirting?'

'Oh, just fluttering your long lashes and doing that little toss of your auburn hair.'

I threw my napkin at Henry and then laughed,

'Well, we both have our ways of sourcing information. The guy in the lounge suit, the only vaguely normal person in the room, is Peregrine's younger brother, Jasper Jerome.'

'Really? Of course, now I come to think of it there is a family resemblance of sorts. His height and … well, nothing more really.'

'Exactly, Jasper is very normal, as I said, and it seems there is not much love lost between the brothers.'

'Ah well, I suppose that's understandable… must be hard to be the spare and not the heir. Anyway, it was a really awful dinner party, wasn't it?'

'Sam and I used to play a game of inviting imaginary guest to dinner. Have you ever played it? For instance, I can just imagine a dinner party with Constable and Gainsborough, wouldn't it be fascinating?' I said dreamily looking into the flames of the fire.

'I can't say I've ever played the game but it's a lovely idea. The thought of getting the two painters to meet over a dinner table. Who else would you invite?'

'Well, we used to make it a rule that guests had to be from the same century so… hmm, 18th century then.'

'Why, we could ask Nelson along then and maybe Napoleon?'

'Do you think that would be a good idea? Isn't it strange to think that they were all alive at the same time?'

'I suppose Gainsborough and Constable would have met.'

'Oh yes, I think they respected each other and were both born in Suffolk, though, of course, Gainsborough was fifty years older.'

'You always say 'of course' when you come out with some fact that not everyone would know.'

'Do I?'

'You do, my love and it's very sweet and non-condescending. I spent hours and hours copying both great masters but never thought much about their lives.'

'So much cleverer to be able to paint. I hope you find time, soon, to get your brushes out again.'

'There will come a time, I'm sure. Who else shall we invite to our fictitious dinner party then?'

'I think we should keep it arty, how about Joshua Reynolds, he would have been around at the time and a leading portraitist.'

'But Nelson would be out of sorts if it was too arty, how about asking Emma Hamilton… she would be good fun.'

'Or poor old Hardy of the kiss-me fame?'

'Could do… but explain the game more…do we get to be there, too?'

'Of course, that's the whole point, Henry.'

'Oh, I see, I mean, I'm sure it would be most enlightening but to be quite honest I'd much rather just have dinner with you and Rosso.'

'Me, too!' I said and Henry stood up and went over to the bed and patted it. 'I think we should go to bed before the bed-warmers cool down.' He turned to me and added, 'If you've had quite enough to eat.?'

I opened the packet of Bourbon biscuits and held it out to Henry,

'Can I tempt you, kind sir? Sir… God, how many times did you say that tonight?"

'Just good manners, my love and yes, definitely you can tempt me.' Henry said, pulling out a long copper bed warmer from the bed and coming over to lay it by the grate. Then, turning quickly he grabbed the packet from my hand and waved it in the air above his head. I made a jump to grab it back but he held it easily out of my reach and backed away from me in the direction of the bed saying, 'Bribery and corruption.'

I jumped at him, encircling my legs around his waist and said, 'You really don't need to bribe me, my love.'

We fell back together into the warmth of the yellow satin bed.

Chapter 12

"I am not always good and noble. I am the hero of this story, but I have my off moments."
P.G.Wodehouse

I awoke slowly, first opening one eye and then the other, blinked and, for more than a minute, wondered wherever I could be. Then, catching sight of a corner of pleated yellow satin, it all came back to me. I pulled the covers over my head as I heard Henry, well, I hoped it was Henry and not some ghostly Jerome, raking the fire. I edged the eiderdown a little and peered out and saw Henry, completely naked, poking the fire into new life. I pulled the cover down a little more as it was a truly entrancing sight. His long back was arched, showing every vertebra, and he was leaning forward and delicately placing a log on a triangular pile that he had laid in the grate. Then, he stood up and looked with satisfaction at the flames leaping up the chimney. I quickly pulled the eiderdown over my head as he turned around.

'It's no good pretending you're asleep, Allie, I know quite well you've been ogling me.'

I pulled the cover back a little and said, 'But you're so oglesome and I do love you so much.'

'Then move over, I'm coming back to bed until the fire burns up a bit. Do you know you've slept in the exact middle of the bed all night?'

'Really? Well, it's that sort of bed with a dip in the middle.' I moved over a little, reluctant to leave the warm patch and Henry jumped in. 'Oh my God, you're freezing, don't touch me!'

'That's not what you said last night, my love. But my hands are hot from the fire… aren't they?'

It was true, his hands were very warm as he ran them over me and soon I didn't feel cold at all.

Our love-making soon made it time for any respectable household to be serving breakfast and as the fire was now burning hot, we finally left our yellow satin nest, braved the cold bathroom and then went down to see if there was anything edible for breakfast.

Rosso greeted us at the bottom of the stairs, accompanied by his Labrador friends. Rosso stood much taller between them and, slowly wagging his long wispy tail, he looked very regal.

'So, Rosso, did you sleep well?' Henry said, patting his head and then paying attention to each of the labradors in turn. Rosso edged between Henry and the labradors, pushing away Henry's hand.

'Better not stroke the Labs, Henry,' I said, tickling Rosso under his long chin, 'You don't want to make Rosso jealous again like yesterday.'

'Dear God, was that only yesterday? It feels like we've been staying here for a week or more. Today, we must see the Constable and go.'

'I agree totally, although I did have a very good night.'

'True but then I was up three times to stoke the fire.'

'Is that a euphemism?' I asked in what I hoped was an innocent voice but before Henry could answer there was a blood-curdling scream from the landing above us. I clutched Henry's arm and squeaked, 'Oh my god, it's the same scream.'

To my surprise and slight annoyance Henry said calmly, 'Exactly the same scream. Haven't you realised it's a recording?'

'A recording' I repeated stupidly, 'What do you mean?'

'Well, personally I don't believe in ghosts, haunted houses or murderous phantom screams, so I took a look behind the curtain in the corridor last night... one of the times when I was stoking the fire for you, no euphemism and no ghost.'

'What do you mean?'

'There's a speaker behind the pelmet of the curtain... obviously something triggers a recording *et voilà* ... the murderous scream.'

'Why didn't you tell me before?' I gave Henry's arm a little pinch before letting go of him, 'I've been terrified.

'No you haven't... you slept soundly all night in the middle of the bed.'

'Well, I still think you could have told me.'

'Are you now going to sulk like Rosso? Honestly, you two are very high maintenance sometimes.'

I rubbed Henry's arm tenderly and said,

'But we are both so worth it and we do love you so very much.'

Rosso seemed to understand and played his part, leaning against Henry and looking up at him fondly.

It was going well but then there was a booming voice behind us and it could only be Sir Peregrine.

'Morning, Morning to you both…how do, how do, what's that? Girlie? Where are you, Girlie, guests for breakfast before we ride out.'

I looked at Henry in desperation and he said quickly,

'Good morning, sir, a ride would be wonderful but we're actually here to take a look at your Constable.'

I thought it was a valiant effort but to no avail… Sir Peregrine was marching ahead, his large tweed jacket swinging loose from his great height and his hands waving wildly above his head… causing the fabulous dusty chandelier to slowly swing.

Chapter 13

> *"I hadn't the heart to touch my breakfast. I told Jeeves to drink it himself."*
>
> P.G.Wodehouse

Breakfast had been endured. I managed a slice of cardboard-like toast and some doubtful jam, possibly marmalade, and Henry downed scrambled eggs on toast as though he actually enjoyed it. Lady Agatha had not appeared, although from time to time Sir Peregrine had bellowed over his shoulder to her as though she might appear,

'Girlie, Girlie are you there?'

I couldn't help thinking that she was very wise to keep out of the way and only wished that I could. Perhaps she was hiding in the warmth of an Aga-ed kitchen? Benson slid in and out of the vast dining hall placing food on the heated salvers on the buffet as though expecting a party of guests. Henry made more valiant efforts to bring up the subject of the Constable but, whether by cunning or lack of interest, Sir Peregrine made no response. Finally, feeling responsible on behalf of my father for bringing Henry to the Hall, I stood up and spoke firmly,

'Sir Peregrine, my father, your friend Edward Ponsonby, asked us to call on you to give an appraisal of your Constable. Would you care to show it to us this morning, because later we really do have to leave?"

Sir Peregrine looked up at me and gave me a horsey smile, 'What's that m' dear You'd like to see our Constable? Nothing simpler but not this morning, I'm afraid. I'm riding over to the Simpson-Brooks to take a look at a filly they have for sale. You should both join me, what's that, wonderful morning. The Constable will still be here when we get back. It's not much of a picture, in my opinion, never cared for it myself, dreary view of a few fields, what?'

Henry stood up now and said,

'Alicia's father, Mr Ponsonby, was under the impression you wanted to sell it. Is that correct, sir?'

'Sell it? What's that? Hmm, never thought about it really. Always hung in the central gallery, don't you know. Might leave a bit of a gap... hmm, no, I don't think we want to sell it.'

I was standing close enough to Henry to hear him smother a sigh and then he said politely,

'Quite, sir, quite right. I completely understand. A family heirloom, no doubt. Sorry about the ride but we should be on our way, but thank you so much for your hospitality.'

Now it was my turn to sigh as I thought of the time we had wasted when we could have been up on the Norfolk coast enjoying a day or so in a comfy pub. I was about to add some version of Henry's little speech, when Lady Agatha entered in a flurry of Hermes silk scarves and accompanied by Rosso and the two labradors.

'Good Morning, Alicia and Henry, do forgive me for not joining you for breakfast but I was tied up in the kitchen with cook planning menus.'

I managed a smile as I thought that I had probably been right about her Aga breakfast and that designing menus was about the worst excuse she could possibly make. Any food that we had been offered since we arrived could, surely, never have been planned. Anyway, our imminent departure was now announced and I felt cheered enough to say,

'Not at all, Lady Agatha, you and Sir Peregrine have been so kind having us to stay but now we really must leave.'

Lady Agatha returned to her habit of wringing her hands together and bending at the waist as she replied,

'Oh, but Alicia, I thought your father said you would take a look at our Gainsborough. He said you work for an auction house in London… that you have quite an important job now.'

I blinked, hoping that when I opened my eyes the whole muddle would have gone away but unfortunately Lady Agatha still stood in front of me, hands clasped together and her face crinkled in concern. I said nothing for a minute, hoping that Henry would say something to sort out the confusion, but for once he seemed to have nothing to say, polite or otherwise. I swallowed and then took a deep breath and said,

'Your Gainsborough? I thought you owned a Constable?' The question was ridiculous enough without continuing to say that I no longer worked at an auction house.

Before Lady Agatha could reply, whether or not she was going to, Sir Peregrine suddenly stood up to his full height, knocking over his coffee cup and yelled,

'Benson! Where the hell's Benson? Can't sit around here all day. Have to do everything myself nowadays. Time to bring the horses round.' He slammed his hand on the table and shouted again, 'Girlie! Tell Benson I'm ready to go.' He pushed back his chair, the carver of the perfect Chippendale set of dining chairs, and it tipped over. Henry leapt forward and caught it just before the pagodo-topped back hit the edge of the iron fender in front of the fireplace.

'Careful, sir!' Henry said, setting the chair on its four elegant chamfered feet and looking at it appreciatively, 'Such a beautiful chair.'

'What's that? Rubbish, gimcrack chairs not built to last… always hated them.'

Henry glanced at me and I just shrugged, feeling quite lost between Gainsborough, Constable and Chinese Chippendale.

Sir Peregrine was now striding down the length of the dining room and making for the door. The two labradors followed at his heels but Rosso looked at Henry and then to me and stayed between us. I stroked his head and said weakly,

'We really can't ride this morning, we don't have any riding clothes with us and…'

Lady Agatha interrupted me, 'Oh, don't worry dear. You can borrow Fenella's togs and Henry is about the same size as Jasper. We can soon find something. Perry will be so very disappointed if you don't go.' She put her arm through mine and continued, 'Do you think you could advise Perry?'

I was close to her now and I could read every line of anxiety in her face.

'Of course,' I said quickly, 'if you show us the Constable… er… or the Gainsborough…we can make a first appraisal and then get a complete authentication arranged.'

Lady Agatha squeezed my arm and said,

'No, dear, no! I meant advice about this filly that Perry is so keen to purchase.'

Lady Agatha was a small, slightly built woman but I felt myself drawn toward the door.

Chapter 14

"There are moments, Jeeves, when one asks oneself, Do trousers matter?"   "The mood will pass, sir.'

P.G.Wodehouse

Sir Peregrine was quite right, it was a wonderful morning for a ride and I could almost have enjoyed it if I hadn't been kitted out in jodhpurs and a hacking jacket at least two sizes too big for me... and then, there were the boots, knee high and gaping around my shins. I was baggily astride a fine thoroughbred hunter and Henry was beside me on another. I turned to him and said in a murderous voice just loud enough to sound over the skittering noise of the hooves on the frosty ground,

'How do you do it? It doesn't matter where we end up... from an Italian beach to deepest Norfolk, you always have the perfect outfit, don't you? I can hardly bear to look at you trotting smugly along in your tailor made kit and handmade boots. You are so infuriating.'

'You look positively adorable, my love, something of the gamin or maybe it's the orphan Annie look? Not sure who she was but...'

I interrupted savagely, 'It's all that stack of Louis Vuitton luggage, isn't it? I bet you have a bag of ski clothes or maybe a wet suit...'

Now Henry interrupted me, 'That's the whole advantage of travelling by car, you must have realised that by now. I can't understand why you lug around that old backpack.'

'It holds all I need.' I replied grumpily, and realising I was losing the argument, I pressed my heels into the sides of my horse and surged ahead in a slow canter, catching up with Rosso who was galloping ahead. As the Norfolk air flew past me, fresh and cold, it was impossible to stay in a bad mood and by the time we had arrived at the farm where the filly was for sale, I was ready to behave well.

'Here we are then!' Sir Peregrine announced rather unnecessarily as we drew to a clattering halt in a cobbled yard. Sliding off his horse he winced as he landed on the cobbles and I looked at him standing there, a riding boot on one foot and an old slipper on the other swollen foot and almost admired him. There was certainly an unstoppable quality to Sir Peregrine Jerome and, as I dismounted I sighed as I remembered I was probably here to stop him from buying an expensive filly. There had been a shadow of desperation in Lady Agatha's wrinkled face as she had beseeched me for help. I remembered, too, that we were only here because my father had said the Jerome's were in dire straits and that the roof needed repair… not that the price of a filly could be anything but a drop in the ocean compared to the cost of repairing the thousands of tiles covering Farley Hall. I sighed and handed my reins to a young lad who had run up to me,

'Thanks,' I said, although I had a sudden desire to jump back on my horse and ride off and away from anything to do with Sir Peregrine.

Then, Henry came around to stand beside me and said,

'Well, you're the art expert so let's see what you can do with horse dealing. Keep it short and sweet, my love, and then perhaps we can get back to why your father sent us into Norfolk.'

'I shall never forgive Pa for this.' I said grimly, pulling up my baggy jodhpurs and looking down miserably at my gaping boots, 'Never ever.'

'Never ever? Honestly, Allie, you sound like a naughty child and… ' He gave a low laugh, 'I must say you look rather like one, too.'

I trod carefully on the toe of his boot and was pleased to see that I had left a dark smudge on the conker-like shine. Rosso, who had been gambling happily around the stable yard, paying his respects to the horses poking their long noses over the half doors, scampered over to me and I leaned over to stroke him.

'Rosso, you understand, don't you?' Rosso wagged his tail and once again my bad mood disappeared. He was that sort of dog, so full of the joys of life that it was impossible not to smile. So, with another heave at my jodhpurs and clumsy in my large boots I went over to join Sir Peregrine who was now talking to the stable lad.

'Morning, young man, we're here to see the filly, what's that?'

The young lad stared at the carpet slipper on Sir Peregrine's foot and then made an effort to reply,

'Yes, sir, but you're expected tomorrow. The master is away in Norwich today.'

'What's that? Simpson-Brook's not here? Ah well, not to worry. Just show us the nag and we'll be off again.'

I signed with relief as obviously Sir Peregrine had confused the appointment and, surely, now we could take a quick look at the horse and get away again.

Henry and Sir Peregrine, were chatting to the lad as they crossed the stable yard and, with a final hitch to my jodhpurs, I followed.

Chapter 15

> *"At the age of eleven or thereabouts women acquire a poise and an ability to handle difficult situations which a man, if he is lucky, manages to achieve somewhere in their later seventies."*
> P.G.Wodehouse

'Well, that was sharp and sweet!'

Henry and I were sitting by the Aga in the kitchen at Farley Hall with Sir Peregrine and drinking hot chocolate.

'I knew by the time the lad had walked her out of the yard that Sir Peregrine shouldn't buy her.'

'Oh, I absolutely agree. I know a bit about polo ponies and a bit less about hunters but she definitely had problems. You didn't pull any punches though. Poor old Sir Perry was decimated.'

'I thought it was the only way to go.' I paused and downed the last of my hot chocolate, then said, 'There was no chance I was going to stand in a freezing field in someone else's clothes and be polite. The filly had such an awkward gait and not one that would improve. Nervous, too, did you see how she shied when I threw down my hat?'

'Oh, I thought that was a bit unfair…certainly made the filly jump. I thought you just did it because you were in a bad temper.'

'Well, I'm not saying I was in a good mood but it's a trick my father used when he bought a pony for me or Sam. Anyway, although Sir Peregrine is not exactly a bad rider, even with a slipper in one stirrup, there's no need to add a nervous horse to his stable. There's no saying who might end up riding him…a guest like us. No, the filly had a wicked look in her eye.'

'Hmm, I agree totally, but you subdued Sir Peregrine magnificently.'

'I only said that my father would never buy the horse and walked out of the field.' Henry began to laugh and I glared at him and added, 'Now what?'

Henry put down his mug of hot chocolate and tried to stop laughing as he said, 'Sorry, but it's a sight I shall never forget, watching you strut off, hitching up your jodhpurs.'

Henry collapsed into laughter and I struggled to be a good sport but it had never been my forte, so I reached out and drank the rest of his chocolate, then said,

'I'm trying to forgive you because I am grateful that you marched straight into the kitchen from the stables and managed to make hot chocolate. It's so nice in here. I wonder where the cook is?'

'Benson said she just comes in from the village now and again.'

'I suppose Benson is now your paid-up puppet? Have you continued to bribe him?'

'Just a little. We had a chat this morning and he told me that he hadn't been paid for two months.'

'Not surprised… they're obviously impoverished. What else did Benson tell you?'

'Apparently the ghostly scream was a wild idea of Jasper Jerome's to keep the Constable safe.'

'What? How does that work? Haven't they heard of burglar alarms?'

'Ah, well that was more gossip from Benson. Apparently a number of great houses in Norfolk were caught in a burglar alarm scam. Some dodgy company from Essex installed quite a few and, believe it or not, the same houses were then robbed.'

'Gosh, maybe Jasper-the-spare is not so crazy then. The scream would certainly stop me from going any further along that corridor.'

'Even a wicked filly like you?'

Henry began to laugh again and I stood up, 'When you have quite finished mocking me, perhaps we could get down to work and see this Constable which may be a Gainsborough. I shall go and change and meet you in the hall in ten minutes.'

I tried to stalk pompously out of the kitchen but the effect was spoiled by the need to hitch up my jodhpurs.

Chapter 16

"Gussie, a glutton for punishment, stared at himself in the mirror."

P.G.Wodehouse

Our bedroom was still delightfully warm as I changed into my own clothes. Rosso had accompanied me and so I enjoyed a little conversation with him while we had some time together.

'You know, Rosso, Henry can be very annoying at times.'

Rosso looked up at me with a mournful face and licked his lips. I carried on,

'He has a knack of being right.'

Rosso made a small nod of his long head and went over to the fire and lay down.

'And how ridiculous it is to have the Alfa boot jam-packed with his luggage. He's such a dandy! I suppose it may be the Italian side of him.'

Rosso curled up in a tight ball and said nothing.

'It's no good you disagreeing, Rosso. It's not very English, is it? I mean, my brother would never be so organised about his clothes. Anyway, whatever you say, it's another side of him always being right and it can be very annoying.'

I looked into the one cheval mirror and admired my own image. I had chosen my best well-fitting Levis and a pale blue cashmere jumper that I had bought in a Hobb's sale. I twisted my hair into a tight topknot and skewered it with a steel blue clip and gave a satisfied nod at my image.

'Come on, Rosso, we can't hang around chatting, let's go. I can't wait to see this wretched Constable-Gainsborough… and, I have to admit, I'm missing Henry already. Ten minutes is quite long enough to remember how much I love him. Do hurry up, Rosso.'

The last words were unnecessary as Rosso was already at the door waiting. I opened it and gave a quick glance toward the curtain at the far end of the corridor. For a moment I was tempted to go toward it and set off the murderous scream but there was a residual feeling of fear in me. I gave a quick shake to my shoulders, feeling cold after the warmth of our bedroom, and turned to the stairs. Rosso, too, had been looking toward the curtain but he turned with me and we raced off and down the stairs to meet Henry.

But Henry wasn't there. I jumped the last few stairs and landed in the centre of the large Bokhara rug and stood still in surprise. Henry was always there, wherever we had arranged to meet… he was always there. I looked around, for a moment wondering if he was hiding and about to jump out at me but there weren't many possibilities. There were more doors than walls and only a round table covered in unopened post, Sir Peregrine's old tweed hat and an urn of wilting flowers. Then, one of the doors opened slowly and I turned to greet Henry but, to my disappointment, Benson appeared.

'Good Morning, Miss Ponsonby, I have a message for you.' He held out a silver salver which I had time to notice was Georgian, with a beautiful fluted rim and delicate engraved floral decoration… in the middle lay a folded piece of paper. I picked it up, expecting to find some joke or trick from Henry but the words were not in his hand-writing.

'Apologies on behalf of Henry, would you join us in the west wing? Benson will direct you. Jasper Jerome.'

I read the message again and then looked at Benson who was standing now with the salver behind his back and staring up at the dusty chandelier. Perhaps he was considering the difficulty of cleaning it as it hung high above us, every crystal…Baccarat, I was almost certain… festooned with cobwebs. This was not the moment for house-keeping and I said sharply,

'I don't understand, Benson. Where's Henry?'

'I believe Count Palliano is in the west wing.'

I was silent for a moment, wondering how Benson knew that Henry was Count Palliano as Henry never used his extinct Italian title. His mother clung to her title as Contessa, even after remarrying but … I stopped myself from thinking further and said,

'Then, you'd better show me the way to the west wing, please Benson.'

Benson gave a small nod, turned on his worn-down heel and Rosso and I followed him through one of the doors out of the hall.

Chapter 17

"There was a sound in the background like a distant sheep coughing gently on a mountainside. Jeeves sailing into action."
                                P.G.Wodehouse

Rosso and I followed Benson along a corridor and then up a staircase, not as grand as the main one but twisting and turning up through several landings and finally arriving at yet another corridor. Benson was breathing heavily by the time we finally arrived at a door at the far end beside a long curtained window. I realised it was a similar reverse version of the corridor of our bedroom and I had a shiver of doubt, almost waiting for another murderous scream to ring out as we approached. There was only the soft sound of our footsteps on the worn Persian runner and Rosso moved without making any noise at all. My heart was thumping in my ears as Benson opened a door and stood back, waiting for me to enter. I put my hand down to Rosso's head and then saw his hackles were raised along the centre of his long back.

'Come on, Rosso,' I said, trying to sound cheerful, 'We'll soon find Henry.'

As I spoke I moved into the darkness of the room and Rosso kept close to me. Then, the door closed sharply behind me.

'Henry?' I called out, my voice sounding very small in the dark shadowy room. There was no answer apart from a shuffling, scraping noise some way from me. My eyes slowly became accustomed to the dark and I turned around, back to the door and tried to open it. Finding it locked I banged on the door panel and then felt for a light switch. Rosso was still at my side but wagging his tail so hard that it brushed against me.

'What is it, Rosso, can you see Henry?'

Now the same sound came again, slightly louder this time and, unable to find a light switch I turned back into the room and edged slowly, very slowly forward. Rosso went ahead of me and I heard him give a happy bark and again the sound of something moving against the floorboards. I took another step forward, my hands outstretched in front of me and stumbled against something heavy and cried out as I stubbed my toe. Suddenly, I remembered the torch on my mobile phone and I quickly pulled it out from my jeans pocket and flashed it around the dark space. Pointing upwards I could make out the heavy beams of an attic room and then, as I moved it down, it lit upon a collection of broken furniture and what appeared to be a clutter of junk and old boxes. I moved cautiously forward and trained the light on the floorboards ahead of me. Then, as the beam moved with me, I was suddenly looking at Rosso and he was standing beside Henry, licking his face. Henry blinked in the torch light but said nothing. He couldn't…he had a length of tape across his mouth and as I moved the beam down I saw he was tied to a chair. I gave a small scream and stayed rooted to the spot. Henry raised his dark eyebrows at me and blinked rapidly. I nearly dropped the phone and as the beam of light jagged to the left I saw that Sir Peregrine was gagged and tied to another chair. His head was slumped forward and he looked horribly dead. Now, Henry was making as much noise as he could through the tape and shuffling his feet on the dusty floor. I came to my senses and ran to him and ripped the tape from his face.

'Good God, Allie, you could have done that a little slower. That hurt!'

'Is that all you can say? It's only packing tape. Do you want me to try and undo the rest of you?'

'If you would be so kind, my love.' Henry spoke in a slow sarcastic drawl and so I left him for a moment and turned to look at Sir Peregrine who was a nasty sight, his mouth hanging open and his long grey hair falling across his face. I was reluctant to touch him and said in a small voice to Henry,

'Is Sir Peregrine dead?'

'No…well, I doubt it. If you could be bothered to untie me I'll take a look at him.'

I bent over and tried to break the strong plastic tape that was wound round and round the whole length of Henry. 'I'm not sure how… I can't break the tape.'

Henry gave a sigh and said, 'Can you find a way into my right hand trouser pocket? There's a penknife in there.'

I ran my fingers down from Henry's waist and found a very small gap between the strips of tape and managed to push my fingers into his pocket. 'This pocket? I can't feel anything except you.'

'Really, Allie this hardly the time and place to play around.'

'I'm not!' I said indignantly, 'I'm just trying to feel for a penknife. Ah, I think I've found it… there's something hard….'

'Allie, behave yourself. I can't believe you're messing around. Any time now Jasper and Agatha may come back and then we'll be in trouble…. Or rather worse trouble.'

'Jasper and Agatha?' I was about to ask more but at that moment I managed to extract Henry's silver penknife form his pocket. I opened it carefully and began to cut through the shiny plastic tape.

'Watch it, Allie, you've just ruined my trouser pocket. Can you work around my hand so that I can cut myself out?'

'Talk about me… how can you worry about your pocket at a time like this?' I moved the knife carefully between Henry's two wrists that were tightly fastened tied behind his back and suddenly his hands were free. 'There, take the knife yourself then.'

Henry took the knife and I stood back as he quickly slashed the tape away from the chair and finally stood up.

'Chinese Chippendale' He said, 'Holding the chair aloft for a moment and inspecting it carefully. 'Just one small section of the trellis back missing… a beautiful chair, one of the set in the dining hall, of course.'

'Henry, are you trying to be annoying or does it just come naturally? Do you think you could tell me just what is going on and perhaps check to see if poor old Peregrine is dead or alive?

Chapter 18

"He had the look of one who had drunk the cup of life and found a dead beetle at the bottom."
                              P.G.Wodehouse

I watched Henry with horrid fascination as he went to Sir Peregrine and rested his hand on his shoulder. It was too dark to see much but I was sure that Sir Peregrine made no movement.

'He's dead, isn't he? Dead!' My heart was beating in my ears again and I felt my knees weaken.

'Don't think so…' Henry's voice was maddeningly calm, almost casual. 'Just knocked out with ketamine or some-such. I'm sure he'll come round.'

'Come round?' I sat down heavily on the Chinese Chippendale chair and held my head in my hands. 'I think I may faint, Henry.'

At this Henry turned his attention to me and said,

'Poor girl, put your head down on your knees. Better not lean back on the chair, don't want to break another one into smithereens.'

I did as I was told and immediately felt better as Henry rested his hand on my shoulder, patted me and took my mobile. Rosso rested his long nose on my lap, licked the back of my hand and sighed deeply in commiseration. I peeped through my fingers as Henry flashed the pale beam from my phone around the dark attic and decided that Rosso was being a lot more sympathetic than Henry. I said in a feeble voice,

'Are you going to tell me what the hell is going on?' I raised my head and stroked Rosso who put his head on one side, waiting for Henry to answer.

'Of course,' Henry said, 'Well, as much as I know. Poor old Sir Perry was bamboozled into leading me up here…' He broke off in mid-sentence and began to open a large trunk that stood in the eaves. 'Looks like dressing-up clothes in here…or something.'

'Henry! Is this the day in your life when you have decided to be thorough annoying. What do you mean bamboozled… bamboozled by whom?'

Henry turned to me and the torch light zig-zagged around as he answered,

'Sorry, my love, are you feeling better now? I thought I'd give you a moment to recover and this place is so fascinating.'

'Fascinating?' I realised I had to stop repeating single words from Henry's pathetic attempt to explain our situation. I stood up and said firmly,

'Enrico di Palliano. Give me back my mobile right now. I'm going to call my brother. As far as I can tell, we are locked in a windowless attic with an unconscious, possibly dead aristocrat. The situation is out of hand and all you can do is callously poke around in the Jerome family's clutter and junk. I've had enough. Give me my phone.'

In the gloom I saw Henry hold out my phone and the light shone for one moment on the dusty floor and then went out.

'Please tell me you turned the torch off, Henry?' My voice was no longer firm but squeaky with fear.

'No, …think the battery's dead. That's not good, is it.' Henry came over and handed me my phone and then put his arms around me. 'Are you all right now, my love?'

'Oh yes, absolutely brilliant. I'm having a great time. Please tell me you have your mobile on you?'

'Sorry, no, you know I hate the thing. Everyone always able to get on to me. I think mine is still in the Alfa. But don't worry, we'll soon be out of here now. I suppose you were bamboozled by Benson, too.'

'If you mean did I do as you asked in your message, then…'

'My note? I never…'

'Benson gave me a message signed by Jasper…'

'Oh, so he's in it, too. I thought the guy that came up behind me was tall.'

'Oh my god, were you knocked out or something?'

'Yes… we were just entering this attic when I caught a glimpse of Benson injecting poor old Perry. He slumped down and then I was clobbered… went out like a light and found myself trussed up on the Chinese Chippendale.'

'Oh my God, so we really have been kidnapped?'

'Not to worry, we'll be all right. They didn't even knock you out or tie you up. Can't think why. Either they have no plan or they're totally inept.'

I tried to agree with Henry's way of thinking but failed and said,

'I don't see why you think we'll be all right. We're locked in and Sir Peregrine needs paramedics or something. He may be dying or.…'

Just as my voice trailed off miserably there was a sound of movement and in the gloom I saw Sir Peregrine raise his head as he said,
'What's that?'

Chapter 19

"Say what you will, there is something fine about our old aristocracy. I'll bet Trotsky couldn't hit a moving secretary with an egg on a dark night."
                                        P.G.Wodehouse

'Well, of course, I realised some time ago that Girlie was playing around with Jasper, what's that.'

Henry had unravelled Sir Peregrine and, even in the gloomy darkness, it was quite obvious that he had come to no harm from being knocked out and tied up. In fact, he seemed in very good humour. Henry and I had been struck dumb by his easy acceptance of the idea that Lady Agatha was not only conducting an affair with his younger brother but that they had stolen the Constable.

'Stolen the Constable?' I said, my voice squeaky with shock, 'But how could they do that? I mean, it's yours, isn't it… a family heirloom and worth a fortune? How could they?'

Sir Peregrine gave a little chuckle, 'I rather believe they'll find out they can't. I suppose that's what all this shenanigans tying me up is all about. They've gone off with it today, what?'

'We must get out of this damned attic.' Henry said and began to pace around, stumbling amongst the debris of junk that littered the floorboards. 'You can't let them get away with it.' He pulled a lighter from his pocket and lit the small flame.

'You have a lighter, Henry,' I said in surprise, 'But you don't even smoke? Why didn't you use it before?'

'Of course, I always have a lighter in my pocket but there's very little gas in it. I didn't use it before because I hadn't found an oil lamp.Now, I have.' As he spoke a small but bright yellow flame pierced the darkness. I moved closer and Henry turned to me and smiled, his white teeth gleaming.

'Henry, you are so wonderful! How clever of you.'

'That's one of the few nice things you have said to me for a long while, my love.'

'I'm sorry,' I said, 'I know I've been in a dreadful mood ever since we arrived.'

'Not all the time, really, dearest, only when you're cold and hungry.'

Now his dark eyes glittered wickedly and I knew he was thinking about our night in the warmth of the yellow satin bed. I sighed and said,

'Well, nearly all the time. I'm so sorry that I'm so horrid and you're so stoically wonderful.'

'Apology completely unnecessary, my love, you're like the little girl in the nursery rhyme, …'when she was good she was very, very good but when she was bad she was horrid.'

There was another chuckle from Sir Peregrine and he recited in a sing song voice, 'There was a little girl, who had a little curl, right in the middle of her forehead. When she was good, she was very good indeed, but when she was bad she was horrid.' By the way, old boy, that's not a nursery rhyme that's a poem by Longfellow, what?'

We both turned to Sir Peregrine and Henry held the oil lamp up higher and in its light we saw that he was dancing in a small circle around a large leathertrunk, his long arms waving.

Henry said very quietly in my ear, 'I believe Sir Peregrine is high. Probably the effects of the Ketamine.'

'Ketamine? What's that?' I muttered back, watching with amusement mixed with dismay as Sir Peregrine repeated the rhyme and began to skip around the attic.

'You must have heard of it… it's a club drug, you must have been warned of the date rape drug?'

'Oh, well, Sam did tell me to always drink directly from a bottle and keep my hand over it.…' I answered vaguely, still bemused by the nimble way Sir Peregrine was skipping around and apparently unaware of his injured ankle, '… but, well, I never clubbed that much, really.'

'Ketamine is a form of anaesthetic and good for pain relief, I believe, I know vets use it legally. One of my polo ponies had an injection once for a swollen fetlock joint.'

'It seems to be working well on Sir Peregrine's fetlock, too.' I said and then added, 'But how did you know it was Ketamine?'

'I could smell it on him. Ghastly sickly sweet smell like cheap fruit sweets… it brought back bad memories of being in the stable when the vet injected my horse. Nearly made me sick.'

'Well, it seems to be having a surprisingly good effect on Sir Peregrine. He's very happy considering his wife seems to have absconded with his brother and his Constable.'

Sir Peregrine was now happily skipping toward us and smiling broadly. I added hastily, 'Are there any bad after-effects?'

'Not sure, well, I don't think so. It's called the k-hole effect by kids who use or rather abuse with it. Possibly hallucinatory, I think.'

'Oh dear, I wish we could get out of here and get him to a doctor or something.'

Sir Peregrine had now found Rosso lying on an old mattress and joined him, slumping down with a happy yawn.

'Do you feel tired, Sir Peregrine?' Henry said sharply, 'I don't suppose you have a key to this attic, by any chance?'

'Key? What's that? Oh, see what you mean, dear boy, but no, not on me, probably to be found in the servant's quarters somewhere.' He waved his long arm around above his head and Rosso settled against him. 'Lovely dog, don't think I've seen you before, old fellow, what's that? Where have the Labs got to, then, what?'

I walked over and said, 'Sir Peregrine, please don't go to sleep and as for you, Rosso, you're not being much help.'

Rosso eyed me balefully and yawned then curled up in a tight ball.

'Dog's damned right, what?' Said Sir Peregrine, also yawning,'Not much we can do, is there. We're banged up in an attic. Someone will find us eventually. Might as well have a kip, what's that?'

'But, Sir Peregrine…' I said, shaking his shoulder a little, 'I thought you said your wife has gone off with your brother and, what's more, stolen your Constable. Don't you care? Don't you want to get out of here?'

Sir Peregrine gave me a horsey smile and said,

'Don't get too flustered, my dear, never does do. Stay calm and everything will be tickety-boo soon enough. Of course, I'm not worried about Girlie. She'll come running back as soon as she finds out Jasper is not as clever as she thought. Couldn't even finish his vet training, what's that? Always a bit of a loser and always, always wanted anything I had. Pure sibling jealousy, I'm afraid. I don't fret over such things. You'll see, they will be back, what.'

Henry joined me and we stood looking down at the long length of Sir Peregrine stretched out at his leisure on the old mattress with Rosso curled up beside him.

'But, Sir Peregrine,' Henry said, 'Surely you can't let them take the Constable?'

'No need to worry, old chap, I had it copied some time ago. Damn good job the bloke made of it, too. The real thing is stored at my bank and so poor Girlie and Jaz have just made off with the fake. Very disappointing for them.'

Sir Peregrine shook his head sadly but then smiled and, with a final 'what's that', he fell fast asleep.

Chapter 20

"Desperate affairs require desperate measures."
Horatio Nelson

'Now what?' I said, turning to Henry and peering into the flickering light of the oil lamp. 'Should we try and keep him awake or something… like when someone has taken too many sleeping pills?'

Henry's face looked doubtful and he moved the lamp aside and turned to look around the attic. 'I think it may be best to let him sleep. Not much else we can do, anyway. Rosso, you lazy dog, no excuse for you.'

Rosso raised his head from the mattress and glared peevishly at Henry.

I said, 'Rosso, it's not our fault we're locked in an attic.'

Rosso turned away and pushed his nose into a fold in the mattress and went back to sleep.

Henry exhaled loudly and said, 'You and Rosso have been taking it in turns to be moody ever since we arrived at this wretched place.' He turned around and added, 'Did you see that huge trunk? It looks ancient.'

'Henry, please, this is not the time to be treasure hunting. We have to get out of here.'

'Hmm, yes, yes indeed we do.' Henry murmured in the distracted way I recognised as not paying attention, and he added 'Hold the lamp a moment, I'll just take a look inside.'

Now it was my turn to exhale loudly as I took the lamp and held it high so that it cast a beam onto the lid of the large leather trunk. Henry ran his fingers over the rusty studs and buckles and then edged it open. I screwed up my nose in disgust at the mouldy smell that rose from inside but Henry carefully opened the lid as far as it would go and put his hands inside.

I closed my eyes, trying to forget all the horror films I had ever seen when a body was found in a trunk. Then blinked and screwed them up tight as Henry said,

'Just dressing up clothes by the look of it and some letters.'

I opened one eye and squinted at Henry who was now carefully pulling out a long coat.

'Looks like a naval great-coat, genuine stuff, not just fancy dress. Just look at the gold braid and epaulets and all the huge buttons.'

'Do I have to?' I said, reluctantly drawing a little nearer with the lamp and holding the collar of my shirt over my nose as Henry laid the coat on the lid of the trunk.

'Look, there's an amazing hat, too!'

'Goodness, it is rather fantastic. It's a bicorne, like the one Nelson wore. I remember seeing one in an exhibition at Greenwich.'

'You're right... it's like the one Nelson is wearing in that gloomy portrait by Leonardo Guzzardi. I went to the Smithsonian around the time they discovered the painting and did an amazing job on restoring it...

showing all the grizzly detail of his war wounds. I was lucky enough to meet the guy involved in working on it and he said that cleaning it was like reverse plastic surgery.'

I shuddered, 'I know the painting you mean. Most portraits lionise Nelson but that one showed the real man and his bravery. Oh, don't Henry!' I cried out in horror as Henry put the hat on his head, 'Don't, it's disgustingly dirty.'

Henry laughed and said, 'Only the dust of ages. I've always admired Horatio Nelson.'

From the darkness behind us, Sir Peregrine's voice called out, 'Quite right! Great man, what's that?'

Henry took off the hat and moved over to the mattress and I held the lamp up again and saw that Sir Peregrine was sitting up with Rosso on his lap.

'Are you feeling better, sir?' Henry said going over to him and leaning down.

'Better? What's that? Nothing wrong with me, never was. I'm fit as a flea. What the hell are we doing in the attic and who the hell are you?'

I sighed and went to join Henry as Rosso stood up and stretched lazily.

'You fell asleep, Sir Peregrine and we're locked in the attic.' I said as sympathetically as I could manage, 'Do you have a key by any chance?'

'Good God, how ridiculous. I know you, young lady, you're the Ponsonby auburn beauty. Never forget a pretty face… but why the hell did you lock us all in the attic? Some sort of prank?'

It seemed impossible to even begin to explain our desperate situation but I was about to make an attempt when the oil lamp gave a little splutter and died out.

Chapter 21

"I could not tread these perilous paths in safety, if I did not keep a saving sense of humour."
Horatio Nelson

'If you hadn't spent so much time messing around with those old dressing-up clothes we might have used the lamp to find a way out of here.' I scowled fiercely at Henry although, in the darkness, it was doubtful he could see me.

'Goodness, you really are in a bad mood, Allie. I did try to break down the door but it's solid oak and bolted on the other side. Do you know, I can feel you glaring at me. I suppose you're cold and hungry?'

'Certainly I am, both and very, very fed up.'

'Here, take my jacket, unless you'd like to wrap yourself up in the old great-coat.'

I knew Henry was teasing me but I reached out gingerly and he passed me his jacket. I knew by the softness of the cashmere and the comforting aroma of Henry's perfume that he hadn't dared to offer me the great-coat. I had been the brunt of my big brother's teasing far too long not to know how far a joke could go. Henry, like Sam, knew my limits of endurance. I pulled on the jacket and then felt Rosso leaning up beside me.

'You're lovely and warm, Rosso, but I bet you're hungry, too.'

'Don't remind him, Allie, or he'll start sulking again. Now, let's see if we can get out of here.'

'There is a small chink of light at the far end...can you see where I mean.' I pointed, but the long arm of Henry's jacket covered my hand and, like scowling, the gesture was useless. I couldn't even see my own hand in the gloom so I moved forward slowly, my hands outstretched in front of me and bumped into Henry,

'Ow, I've bumped my nose now. Why were you standing in the way, Henry?'

'In the way? Sorry, my love, but quite honestly I wish you'd cheer up a bit.'

How can I when...'

Sir Peregrine's voice interrupted me and it was coming from just behind my right ear.

'Now then kiddiwinks, enough of this banter, best keep a sense of humour, what's that? I'm sure Benson will find us soon.'

'Benson?' Henry's voice came close to my left ear and I could tell he was striving to keep patient as he replied sourly, 'I think you can forget any idea that Benson will come to your aid, Sir Peregrine. He was playing us all for fools. He's part of the plot to steal your Constable, I'm afraid.'

'What's that?'

I sighed thinking that I was truly standing between two most annoying men. I put my hand down and felt for Rosso. He was standing right beside me and I rested my hand on his long narrow head and sighed again.

'Rosso, how lovely it is that your head is the perfect height for my hand to rest upon. Now, let's try and find a way out of here.'

Rosso licked my hand and we walked slowly forward together and toward the slanting chink of light that I had noticed at the far end of the long attic room.

Sir Peregrine said,

'Benson a bad apple, what's that? Good God, been with me for years. I know he's rather one for the horses and takes money off our guests now and then … but … '

'Hmm, well, I suppose he just reached rock bottom. Maybe has gambling debts?'

'Could be, could be.' Sir Peregrine's voice sounded a little further away as he continued chatting to Henry in the pitch dark, 'Did I hear you say you found Nelson's great-coat?'

'Well,' Henry laughed as though enjoying a cosy chat, 'Not the real thing, of course, but it looked vintage.'

'No, that will be Nelson's all right. My old Grandpops had rather a penchant for our local here, Horatio Nelson, don't you know. Collected memorabilia, what's that, letters and medals and there was mention of a coat. One he wore at the Battle of the Nile, so we were told when we were children… used to play up here with Jasper. Good times, what's that?'

I had nearly reached the shaft of light that glinted through a small gap in the rafters but I was still near enough to hear Henry draw in his breath sharply and then say,

'You mean, sir, Nelson's actual coat?'

Before I could call out that perhaps they could chat another time about Horatio Nelson when my toe struck hard into something metallic and by the sprinkle of icy water that I could feel on my legs I realised it was a bucket of water. Rosso, too, jumped back as the water sprayed onto his paws. I called out in dismay,

'Oh no, this is too much, now I've bumped into a bucket of icy water. Henry, do something!'

I heard Henry shuffling toward me in the dark as he called back,

'Stay still, my love and I'll find you.'

I leant down to brush the water from my jeans and Henry bumped into me from behind, nearly tipping me forward.

'Henry! Look out! You nearly knocked me over.'

'Sorry, sorry, I have you now! I'd recognise that little bottom anywhere.' Henry gently patted my behind and then moved his arms around my waist. I stood up straight and leaned back against him.

'I've had enough, Henry. Now Rosso and I have been splattered with icy water. There's a bucketful just in front of me.'

'Excellent!' Henry replied, causing me to almost growl with anger. Then he continued, 'Look up, look up, Allie! There's a gap in the rafters… there's a chink of daylight.'

'I know, that's what I saw from the other end of the attic. There must be a leak in the roof. I really can't see what's excellent about that.'

'It may be a way out of here. I could get up and make the hole larger and get out on the roof.'

'Are you completely insane? How on earth do you think you can even reach up there let alone climb through and onto the roof?'

'Stay right here and I'll be back in a mo.'

I decided not to reply as it was so obvious that I would stand still, not knowing if there was another bucket just waiting for me to step into. Rosso moved away with Henry and I heard a great deal of dragging and shifting noise behind me.

'Do not bump into me again Henry. What the hell are you doing?'

Henry's voice came close to my ear again as he said,

'I've dragged the trunk over here and a chair. I can climb up if you just steady the chair a bit.'

'Are you serious? There's no point. It's just the smallest gap and… ' Before I could say any more, Henry had knocked over the bucket and water was streaming around me. 'Now look what you've done.'

'Better an empty bucket, don't you think? Now, can you feel the edge of the trunk in front of you?'

'My fingers are so icy, I'm not sure I can feel anything.' I sounded very grumpy, even to myself and there was an unpleasant ring of self-pity in my voice. I heaved a long sigh and then reached forward and felt the rounded edge of the leather trunk. 'OK, yes, I can feel the edge. Now what?'

'Good, now feel forward over the top and you should find the legs of the chair… lovely Chinese scroll feet… do you have hold of them?'

'I can't believe you're still talking antiquese… but yes, I can feel two feet… Chinese or otherwise.'

'Excellent! Now just hold them steady while I climb onto the chair. The top of the trunk is rounded so it's not so easy to balance.'

'Henry, if you fall and break your neck there is still no way out of here. It's too dangerous.'

But as I spoke I could feel the two feet of the chair rock and I gripped them hard, steadying them.

'It's fine, 'Henry's voice came from above me, 'Just keep hanging on as I'm going to try and prise one of the rafters a bit.'

To my horror, the chair began to wiggle and I sat on the trunk in order to get a better grip. I was about to shout at Henry to come down when a bright shaft of white light fell over me. I looked up and saw Henry stretching up and moving a plank that rested on the rafter above his head.

'I can see you!' I called out in excitement, the relief of not being in the dark making me forget for a moment to hold the chair. It slipped off the trunk and fell to the floor with a loud clatter. I looked up again and saw that Henry was now clinging to one of the rafters. He looked down at me and I could see his teeth flashing one of his best dental advert smiles, then he said casually,

'Do you think you could get the chair back on the trunk, and don't forget it is a priceless Chippendale, my love that is, if your hands are not too cold?'

I hurriedly dragged the chair back onto the trunk and stood it back under Henry's feet.

'Thank you, well done! Now I think I can make a bigger gap…'

Sir Peregrine suddenly spoke from behind me,

'I say, what an amazing bloke you are, Henry, what?' He sat down heavily on the end of the trunk and added, 'Who'd have thought of that, eh? Entire roof is like a damned sieve, you know.'

In the bright light that now fell over us, I looked at Sir Peregrine and said,

'Hmm, I have to agree, he is an amazing bloke.'

Chapter 22

"Unseen in the background, Fate was quietly slipping lead into the boxing-glove."
P.G.Wodehouse

Unfortunately, try as he might, Henry just could not open up the gap between the rafters wide enough for him to climb through.

'The laths are solid oak and resting on thick oak beams. I thought with the rain and snow coming through there would be some rot but I can't budge anything.'

'Do come down, Henry, please. The chair is so wobbly.'

'Hold it tighter for a second. I'm going to pull myself up so that at least I can poke my head out.'

I gripped the chair legs as Henry gave a small jump and heaved himself up to cling to a cross beam.'

Rosso gave a small anxious bark and I said,

'You're quite right, Rosso, Henry has gone into heroic mode now.' I looked up at Henry's long legs dangling loose and if it hadn't been terrifying it would have been funny. 'Come down, Henry, I'm holding the chair, please, come down. There's no point in looking out.'

Henry made no answer, possibly he couldn't even hear me with his head poking through the small opening and into the cold outdoors. I exhaled loudly and then added,

'OK, so what can you see?'

Henry's voice came down to me as though from a mountain top,

'Fantastic view, panoramic. I can see the sea!'

'Really? I thought we were in the depths of the Norfolk countryside. What else?'

'A huge orchard to the west and a deer park, acres of fields but well-wooded and I can see two lodge cottages and the perimeter walls.' Henry shouted louder, 'All your land, Sir Peregrine?'

'What's that?' Sir Peregrine had been sitting on the trunk, stroking Rosso and seemed surprised at the question, 'Why, of course, my land for just about as far as you can see even from up there. What? Can you see a chimney?'

'What was that?' Henry asked, shifting his clutch on the beam and swinging from one hand as he lowered his head and looked down at us. 'What's that?'

I almost closed my eyes not wanting to watch Henry swinging unconcernedly high above me while apparently 'what's that' was now contagious?

'A chimney.' Sir Peregrine shouted louder.

'Oh, yes, I'm within a yard or so of a chimney. Fine Elizabethan stack, square, of course, and built to resemble a classical column… not the earlier Tudor corkscrew pattern.' Henry swung from one hand to the other and added in his most annoying casual voice, 'In fact, there's a cluster of three chimneys almost within my reach.'

'Henry,' I called up loudly in frustration we do not need a lecture on architecture. Will you please come down before you slip.'

'Hold the chair steady then, I'll come down, nothing more to do up here.'

I grabbed the chair legs and Sir Peregrine reached out to help as Henry's feet felt for the chair seat and then landed. I sighed with relief as Henry sat on the chair and smiled at me, saying, 'Well, I'd better have another go at the door but your hair clip was no good in the lock.'

Sir Peregrine patted Henry on the back and said, 'Well, you tried your best, young fellow. Couldn't do more. Pity, because I believe most of the chimneys have some sort of ladder on one side.'

Henry looked at Sir Peregrine with interest, 'Oh, of course, yes, I'm sure you're right. I've seen that sort of arrangement before… in fact, at school once, I had a lark with some friends and we climbed the chimney using some fixed rungs in the brickwork.'

'Really, what school was that?' Sir Peregrine looked sharply at Henry and added, 'In Italy, I suppose?'

'No, no, I went to Eton, sir.'

'Well, well, me too for my sins. Years ago now. I used to go up to the Bullingdon Club for dinner but haven't been there for an age. In fact, I haven't been anywhere for a long time…don't see the point, what's that?'

'Well, I can see you have everything you need here, sir, but I suppose you should get the roof seen to at some point?'

They carried on chatting as though we were sitting in front of a log fire and sipping cups of tea. I stroked Rosso and my ears began to buzz as I ignored their conversation and realised what I had to do. My heart was racing and I no longer felt cold as I looked up at the gap in the roof above me.

Chapter 23

"England expects that every man will do his duty."
Horatio Nelson

We had argued long and angrily but finally I had won. Now, was the moment that I regretted the whole idea. I was standing on Henry's shoulders as he stood on the chair with Sir Peregrine steadying it. Rosso had begun to whimper and dash anxiously around the trunk. My head and shoulders were out in the cold fresh air and, I had to agree with Henry at this point, it was a fantastic panoramic view. I managed to slip my right arm through and it rested uncomfortably against the icy sharp edge of a roof slate. I wriggled a little around and brought my left arm through and then eyed the chimney to my left. It was not more than a yard away, as Henry had said but the distance was not the point. Between me and the chimney was a steep slope of evil dark slates, slippery as an ice rink…in fact, I noticed there were patches of ice between the edges. I knew this was my deciding moment as I couldn't bear the cold for too long. I spread my arm as wide as I could and pulled myself up until the rafter opening cut into my waist. Henry had torn up an old curtain and fashioned a rope of sorts to tie around me and now, as I wriggled myself further out the knot of the curtain jammed. I squirmed around and then, rather too suddenly, I slipped through, stifling a small scream of fear. Our idea was that I would cling to the curtain as I edged along to the chimney. As with many hurriedly planned ideas it now didn't seem a very good one. The roof sloped steeply and I thought that the old slates would possibly dislodge and slide to the ground below… a long way below. I then made the mistake, ignoring Henry's warning, of looking down. I had to close my eyes for a moment as giddiness swamped over me. It was hopeless and I decided I would have to wriggle back down again and into the attic and Henry's arms. I opened my eyes and exhaled, my breath forming a freezing cloud in front of me. Then, I thought about something that I had seen before I had felt too dizzy to look. I risked looking down again and there it was… a parapet or wide gulley, perhaps only a couple of yards below me. Could I slide down and then walk along it to the chimney? It certainly looked less dangerous than trying to move diagonally up and across to where the chimney stood against the tiles. I bit my lip, trying to decide and then looked again at the square edge of the chimney. Where was the ladder that Sir Peregrine had mentioned? I was freezing cold and yet a trickle of perspiration ran between my breasts and I was breathing fast. I thought of Sam and his brotherly advice when he had taught me to rock climb in a gym. Breathe slowly and concentrate on the next step. I heard his voice in my ear but it was of little use as not only could I not control my breathing but I had no idea what next step I should take. Most of my brain was telling me to wriggle back down through the hole in the roof but there was a niggling thought that stopped me. Then what? Locked in the attic with no-one knowing we were there? No mobile, no-one even missing us? I made up my mind and shouted down to Henry,

'It's going to be easy. Hang on tight to the curtain, you may need to take my weight.'

Before he could answer or question me and before I thought about it any more, I pulled myself right through the gap and hung onto the edge, my body spread out on the slope of the roof. I had a ridiculous brief thought that I was ruining Henry's jacket but, underneath, my favourite blue cashmere jumper might escape too much damage. Then, the curtain edged through and I had a close up view of the faded silk brocade as I rested my face against it and slowly edged down the tiles. My feet could make no purchase so I relied on the curtain, hand over fist, inching down and down. I risked another peep below me and saw that I had nearly reached the narrow parapet. My feet dangled uselessly above it and then the curtain stopped and I was stuck.

'Let out a bit more curtain, Henry!' I yelled and then looked back up to see that Henry was looking down at me, his head out of the roof hole, his eyes wide with shock.

'I'm nearly down on the parapet. Give a bit more curtain,'

Henry made no reply but somehow edged a little more length and my toes touched the guttering and then I was standing on the narrow parapet. I wanted to sink to my knees with relief but the curtain was stretched taut. Either I had to undo the knot around my waist or… or nothing, I realised with a sinking heart as I looked at the chimney looming above me. My fingers, numbed with the cold, pulled uselessly at the knot.

'I can't undo the knot, Henry.' I shouted without daring now to look up or down. Henry answered very calmly,

'You're doing very well, Allie. Don't try to untie it. I'll have to let go of my end and you can slowly draw it down. When you reach the chimney you could tie it to the ladder.'

'OK,' I answered feebly, not at all sure that I could do any such thing… or that there was a ladder. Then, the silk curtain slithered down to me, catching on a slate and finally coiling up at my feet. I carefully began to wind it, the way my father had taught me to wind a rope in a figure of eight around my hand and elbow. I felt strangely calm for a moment and, holding the curtain under my arm, I edged slowly along the parapet to the chimney. Henry was right, I thought crazily, the style was of a classic column and I clung onto the thought as though it mattered. Finally, I reached the edge of the stack and clasped it tightly for a moment. It was so much larger that I had imagined and I stretched out to feel around to the back. I gave a small squeak of relief as my fingers found a metal rung. I stood up again and unfurled the curtain and found the end and wrapped it twice around the rung and then tied a tight clove hitch knot, whispering thanks to my brother again for his early teaching. I had never wanted to be a Girl Guide but

Sam was mad about the Boy Scouts and would return from some camp or another and insist on teaching me all that he had learnt. It was comforting to think about Sam and I could feel tears clouding my eyes as I gave the knot a final tug.

'This won't do.' I said firmly to myself and began to feel for the end of the rung. Somehow, being tied to a chimney made me feel more secure although I knew it was ridiculous. If I fell and swung on the end of a silk curtain it wouldn't be too good. If only it wasn't so very cold, I thought, or maybe said aloud. The iron rung was icy in my grip but I could feel the far end when I stretched and it was securely attached to the masonry. I slid one foot tentatively around the stack and, clinging tight to the rung, I easily found another rung below. It was a ladder. My heart was beating fast and I told myself to stay very calm, not to hurry. I was three floors up from a stone terrace and I had to move slowly. I swung my other foot around and now I was standing against the chimney. I reached my right foot down and felt another rung easily in reach. So, I could descend but now the problem was the curtain. I tugged on my own knot and managed to untie it. The silk slithered down beside me as I took a step down and then another. I shouted up to Henry,

'I've found the ladder. I'm going down. It's easy now.'

His voice came back to me but too far away to make out his words. I hoped he had heard me and then concentrated on moving slowly down, keeping the wretched length of curtain to my right hand side.The rungs were treacherously slippery and once or twice in the descent there was a rung missing but, finally, I made it down to the icy flagstone terrace.

Chapter 24

"Thank God, I have done my duty."
Horatio Nelson

My first thought was to race back inside and go to tell Henry that I was safe. Then I remembered that Sir Peregrine had said something about keys being kept in the servants' quarters. I ran along the terrace, jumping over clumps of frosty moss and skidded to a halt at the main front entrance only to find the doors locked. Not waiting to think about how that had happened I ran back and around the e-shaped building, my breath rasping in the cold air. Finally, at the rear of the huge building I found a solid gate marked 'Servants' Entrance' and to my utter relief it opened easily. There were a few steps down and then another door which hung open. I ran inside and found myself in a long boot room hung with hunting jackets and strewn with boots and walking sticks. There was another door at the far end and, once again it opened easily. As soon as I was through I was met by the two black labradors who greeted me enthusiastically, barking and half-jumping in delight.

'Hello, boys!' I spoke but my voice was dry and croaky. There was a large butler's sink under the window and I went to it and quickly drank from the tap. The water was as icy cold as everything I had recently encountered but it was deliciously refreshing. I spotted an empty dog's bowl on the floor and filled it. The Labs could hardly wait for me to place it on the flagstone floor before they hustled each other to drink greedily.

'So, you've been locked in, too, have you?'

They made no reply but carried on noisily lapping the water but at least my voice sounded more like my own. I left them to it and hastily looked around for a row of hooks or any possible place for keys to be stored. There was a very large plank along one wall with a row of ancient brass bells, each marked with a room, but nothing marked attic. I sighed thinking, of course, it would be unlikely. I began to pull open the drawers in a shabby dresser that stood against the opposite wall and rooted around amongst old paperwork, mostly bills and recipes. No attic keys. The Labs had finally finished drinking so I shooed them outside and then went through another door into what seemed to be a back kitchen. Right in front of me was a row of hooks and, amongst some old aprons I found a bunch of keys. I grabbed them and called to the Labs who came blundering back to join me as I went through yet another door and found myself in the blissfully warm kitchen. It seemed impossible to believe that it was only earlier that day that Henry had made me hot chocolate and we had sat at the long table. I was drawn to the Aga and rested my hands on the tea towels that hung along the front bar for a moment. Then, I said firmly.

'Right lads, let's go and rescue your master and mine and your new doggy friend, Rosso.'

As though they understood me, they hurtled out of the kitchen and I decided it would be best to follow.

They were retrievers, I hoped, as they dashed into the main hall and skidded to a stop under the chandelier.

I tried to think which way Benson had led me out of the hall. There were six doors to choose from and all I recalled was that he had told me that Henry was waiting in the west wing. But where was west exactly? Had the staircase been on my left…or my right? The symmetry of the hall was confusing. I turned in a circle, thinking how long it could take to find the attic if I made a mistake from the beginning. I spotted Sir Peregrine's old hat lying on the round table beside the vase of wilting flowers. I snatched it up and thrust it under the noses of the Labs. They sniffed it obligingly and wagged their tails but I had little hope that my idea would actually work. Both dogs whimpered slightly and then made for the door to the right of the staircase. Had I under-estimated them and were they actually leading me to their master? I opened the door and the dogs dashed ahead and I ran after, remembering, now, that Benson had led me up a winding staircase… and already the dogs were thundering up and up above me … my hopes were raised and I called out,

'Good boys, good boys, seek, seek!' Hoping that words of encouragement would help but they were set on a course and took no notice of me as we reached a top landing and I found myself in a long corridor.

'This is it!' I said, as the Labs had now drawn to sudden halt and were sniffing at the worn Persian runner. Then, whimpering and snuffling they were off again and had reached an oak door and had already begun to scratch at it before I joined them.

'Henry, Henry!' I yelled as loud as I could and immediately and wonderfully, I heard him call out my name.

Chapter 25

"First gain the victory and then make the best use of it you can."
Horatio Nelson

'I should have guessed the Labs would rescue us.' Sir Peregrine was seated close to the Aga in the kitchen, knocking back a large glass of brandy. The Labs were spread out at his feet and Rosso, lying alongside raised his head and looked at Henry.

'Well, sir,' Henry began as he stirred cups of hot chocolate, 'I think Allie had something to do with it. I am never going to be able to forget watching her skittering down that icy slate roof.' He passed me a cup of chocolate and gave me a smile so tender that it would have sold supermarkets clean out of all brands of toothpaste.

'Thank you,' I said, attempting to look heroically modest, then added, 'Gosh, it's too hot in here.' I threw off Henry's jacket which had lost most of its buttons and had a torn lapel and passed it to him.

'I never thought to hear you say that, my love…too hot?'

'Oh, I think I'm a different person altogether. My blood is up now and I'm not even afraid of heights.' I sipped the creamy chocolate and said, 'I still like hot chocolate the way you make it, Henry.'

'So glad, though to be truthful I had trouble grating the chocolate my hands are still shaking so much. I think I'm in shock. I have never felt so useless as when you disappeared out of that damned hole in the roof.'

'Not even that time in the Loire?

Henry noticeably shuddered and said,

'That was grim, no need to remind me. I think we should give up this antique-hunting lark and I'll go back to peacefully painting water-colours.'

Sir Peregrine had finished his brandy and was looking sadly into the empty glass. At Henry's last words his head shot up.

'What's that? You're a painter chap… artist what?'

'Well, yes, I dabble but now I'm working in the family antique business, Palliano's.'

'What, Pally-whatsits? Eyetie family, heard your name somewhere. Maybe Girlie mentioned you.'

I decided it was time to get back to reality, never easy with Sir Peregrine on one end of the conversation. But I had to try if we were ever to get away from Farley Hall.

'We came to value your Constable, Sir Peregrine.'

'Aha, that fooled you then, don't you remember I told you it's in the bank vault? You're a lovely lass, young Ponsonby, brave as a young lion, too, but you must try to concentrate. I told you the Constable's in the bank, what?'

I sighed and tried more hard truth,

'Indeed, Sir Peregrine, but if you remember, your wife and your brother have absconded with…' I faltered to a halt as, of course, they hadn't stolen the real Constable at all and I didn't want to told off again.

'Dearie me, going to be rather a blow to them both when they find out it's a copy. Expect they thought to live together on the proceeds. It's been on the cards for years.'

'I see,' I said feebly and looked to Henry for support. He shrugged, one of my favourite rather Gallic-Italianate shrugs of his broad shoulders and said,

'Well, sir, do you want us to value your Constable another time, perhaps?'

'Good idea, what, never liked the thing, rather a dark muddy daub in my opinion, what's that? Now, the Gainsborough is another kettle of fish. Pretty little picture.'

'So,' I said, sitting up straight, 'So you do own a Gainsborough, too? Is it a family portrait?'

'No, no, we have plenty of those around the place. The Gainsborough is a landscape, what's that, you know, lovely trees and a bit of a river with a few peasant lads fishing.'

Henry was also looking attentively at Sir Peregrine and Rosso stood up as though ready for action.

'Would you show it to us when you've recovered a little, sir?' Henry said politely and Sir Peregrine clapped his hands and guffawed with laughter, causing the Labs to stir and look up at him.

'What's that, young Henry? Show you the Gainsborough? Glad to. But it's in the bank rubbing shoulders with the Constable. Have to make an appointment.' Sir Peregrine seemed to register our disappointment and added, 'Tell you what, why not take a proper torch up to the attic? You may find some other interesting junk up there... those relics of Nelson and I think there's something my mother always called the Gainsborough Box.'

Henry and I both stood up quickly in excitement and I'm sure we were both about to ask more but just then a telephone rang from somewhere in the distance.

'Should you answer that, Sir Peregrine?' I said as it rang on and on,'Do you want me to answer it? Where is it?'

'No idea, young Ponsonby, no idea, what! I'm sure Benson will answer it eventually.'

Henry and I looked at each other helplessly as Sir Peregrine leaned back in his chair and fell fast asleep.

Chapter 26

> *"Time is everything; five minutes make the
> difference between victory and defeat."*
> Horatio Nelson

The phone rang on and on and the Labs stood up lazily, stretched and lumbered out of the kitchen with Rosso in tow.

'I do believe they know where the phone is, Henry. You know, they really are amazing at finding stuff. I could've taken hours to find the right attic without them. There are so many staircases. The Labs were amazing, just sniffed Sir Peregrine's old hat and off they went.'

Rosso had just reached the door as I finished speaking and he turned and gave me the most reproachful look that a dog can give. I carried on hastily,

'Of course, they're not highly intelligent like Rosso… just well-trained to hunt and live up to their name.'

'Labrador?' Henry followed me as we made for the door, 'How do they live up to the name of Labrador.'

'No, Labrador Retriever, the retriever bit, I meant.' We were still uselessly arguing the point when we reached the main hall and found both Labs sitting down by a telephone. Henry moved forward quickly and snatched off the receiver

'Hello, Farley Hall.'

His voice was very serious and I amused myself for a moment imagining Henry as an elegant young Jeeves when I saw a look of shock on his face. I moved forward and pulled at Henry's hand so that I could listen in. A woman's voice was saying,

'So, eventually the man gave this number. They are both in A & E but can be picked up any time now. Fortunately they only suffered minor injuries.'

'I see,' Henry said, grimacing at me as I tried to wrestle the phone from him. 'I'll tell Sir Peregrine immediately he returns and call you back if I may.'

'Very well, the police will want to speak to Sir Peregrine Jerome as the car was licensed in his name.'

'I see,' Henry said again, 'I'll inform him of that, too. Are they not able to drive themselves away from the hospital?'

'Goodness, no… the car was burnt out. The couple have been extremely lucky.'

'I see,' Henry said yet again although there were a hundred questions I could have asked.

'Very well, I'll leave it to you then.' The woman's voice sounded slightly impatient or at least hurried. 'They both burnt their hands trying to retrieve something from the boot of the burning car so they couldn't drive anyway. Please arrange for them to be collected as soon as possible as we are extremely busy here.'

'Of course, of course. I'll get on to it directly. King's Lynn hospital and…'

Before Henry could finish the line was cut.

'Goodness!' I said, 'They didn't get far then and both with burnt hands. It's horrible. They must have been trying to save the Constable.'

'Or rather the fake Constable, but of course they didn't know that. Don't you think Sir Peregrine is quite a wily old bird?'

'Oh yes, all that bluster and what's that's is rather a front, I think. It seems he knew all about Jasper and Lady Agatha having an affair. He doesn't seem too worried.'

'When we were waiting in the attic he told me about them. In fact, he told me that Jasper had always wanted everything he had and as far as he was concerned he thought Lady Agatha, his Girlie, would be better off with Jasper. Then, to my shock, he told me he was happier with the cook!'

'Happier with the cook? Whatever do you mean?' I stared at Henry in amazement.

'Long term affair apparently.'

'Good God, it just gets worse and worse. I shall never forgive my father for sending us into this mess.'

'Hmm, well, there is the real Constable to be considered now…'

'I know, it really is very exciting. I remember some years ago that Christie's sold a large oil painting by Constable for over twenty-two million… it was in a series of large scale paintings of the Stour Valley. Imagine if it's anything like that.'

'I like the way Sir Peregrine called it a muddy daub! Then, there's all the attic to explore. Do you think the Gainsborough box could possibly be…'

'One of Gainsborough's light boxes with paintings on glass?' I interrupted Henry and we clutched hands together in the sheer excitement of the hunt.

'Then, there's that trunk full of …'

'Surely dressing up clothes. That bicorne hat and coat can't possibly be Nelson's, surely?

The two Labs rose to their feet and wagged their tails as Sir Peregrine appeared in the hall,

'I think you'll find it's the kit that Horatio wore at the Battle of the Nile. I thought I told you that my old grandfather was a bit of a Nelson buff and he bought anything he could lay his hands on… old letters, mostly. As a child I remember the day Grandpops came back with the hat and coat. There was some row about it, too, something was missing and then later found, but it cost a small fortune and my Mama was not well pleased.'

Henry and I stared at Sir Peregrine as he rambled on and then suddenly I remembered the phone call. I think Henry remembered at exactly the same time and we turned to each other, probably both hoping that the other would begin. I bit my lip and nodded at Henry. He was always so diplomatic at this sort of thing and I had no idea where to begin.

Henry drew in a long breath and then said quietly,

'There was a phone call, sir, nothing to be too alarmed about but it was from King's Lynn hospital. Apparently Lady Agatha and Jasper had some sort of car accident and were taken to outpatients. They've been treated for burns on their hands as they had attempted to get something out of the boot when the car caught fire. But they can't be too bad as they're ready to be discharged. Apparently the car is a write-off so someone has to pick them up... or arrange something?'

I thought Henry had explained matters very well although he tailed off rather at the end. I looked anxiously at Sir Peregrine, wondering if he had the gist of the matter. To my surprise, Sir Peregrine gave a small version of his usual full-throated guffaw and said,

'Dear dear, burnt their fingers and their boats by the sound of it and all for a muddy fake, what? Something unpleasantly like Arabic justice, what? Well, I can't send Benson, what's that, wonder what would be best?' Of course, I knew what was coming next...'Unless, you and young Ponsonby here would go pick them up? You have your Alfa, what's that?'

Chapter 27

"We see nothing until we truly understand it.'
                                                    John Constable

Sir Peregrine had posed his question and then ambled back in the direction of the kitchen as though it was all arranged. I looked at Henry in dismay.

'I don't understand… I mean, his wife goes off with his brother and steals two valuable paintings and Sir Peregrine just wants them picked up? I mean… surely…'

Henry gave a small laugh and said, 'I don't think Sir Peregrine is to be understood, my love. He lives by his own standards, I suppose.'

'But Henry, you're not honestly thinking of going to King's Lynn hospital?'

'Good Lord, no! We only have enough in the battery to get us to the coast and the next charging station. Anyway, do you really think I would drive across Norfolk to pick up a guy who clobbered me and then tied me up? I wouldn't mind giving him a light punch on the nose when we next meet though.'

'True, so true and I'm very glad you think that. I thought you might go all Eton gent and say you'd go. But what to do then?'

'I'll find my mobile, I think it's in the Alfa. I have the number of a taxi company and I'll arrange for them to be picked up.' He went toward the front door and then turned back to me with and gave me a wicked smile, 'No real need to hurry, is there? Won't hurt the absconding duo to wait awhile. Coming with me, Rosso?'

Rosso looked up at me and the Labs copied him and I shook my head and said,

'Go on, all of you, you need some air. Off you go!'

Rosso nudged my hand then galloped across the hall with the Labs thudding after him and I watched until the door closed behind them. I was pleased that Henry had decided to send a taxi and I thought I would go and tell Sir Peregrine... if he was awake.

The warmth of the kitchen met me but there was no sign of Sir Peregrine. I sighed and thought that I didn't even have the Labs to help find him. I wandered back to the hall and across into the room where we had taken drinks. I had the idea that Sir Peregrine, would be in search of some form of alcohol. I pushed open the door quietly and peered into the shadowy vast room. The fire no longer glowed and it took me a while to realise that Sir Peregrine was sitting in a wing chair looking at Benson who was standing in the middle of the room and pointing a small pistol straight at Sir Peregrine. I froze, and stayed completely still, not sure if I had been heard or not. Benson was shouting in a high-pitched, desperate voice,

'Just give me the key, give me the bloody key!'

Sir Peregrine made no answer and I crept into the room and, as my eyes became adjusted to the gloom, I spotted the wooden coat hanger that I had left on the chair... was it really only yesterday? I edged forward and Benson was still screaming, repeating the same words and waving the pistol wildly. Suddenly, Sir Peregrine spotted me and his eyes widened in shock and I knew I had to act fast. I leapt forward and grabbed the coat hanger and swung it wide and hit Benson hard on the back of his neck. He fell to the ground and the pistol went off with a sharp bang. I stood still, rooted to the spot in horror and then the door opened behind me and Rosso galloped into the room and came to me. He was quickly followed by the Labs who went straight to Sir Peregrine. Then, to my utter relief, Henry was beside me.

'What the hell…' He put his arms around me and I felt my knees begin to give way but I managed to stutter,'

'I've killed Benson, he's dead.'

Henry almost carried me to a sofa and Rosso sat beside me. I hugged him close as Henry ran to Benson who lay perfectly still on the floor. First, Henry picked up the pistol and slipped it into his pocket, then he knelt beside Benson. He stood up and looked at me,

'Not dead, just knocked out I should say.' He gave Benson a nudge in the ribs with the toe of his shoe. Benson groaned and muttered,

'Give me the key.'

I sat up on the sofa, immediately feeling better and said,

'He was pointing the gun at Sir Peregrine and…'

Henry went to where Sir Peregrine was still sitting in the wing chair and now happily stroking the Labs.

'Are you all right, Sir Peregrine?' Henry asked, resting his hand on Sir Peregrine's shoulder.

'What's that? Me? I'm all right, dear boy, saved by the Labs again, what?'

Henry gave a small sigh of exasperation and came over to me,

'I heard a pistol shot, Allie, whatever happened?'

'I coat-hangered Benson and the pistol went off as he fell so…' I stood up and looked around the room, 'Oh goodness, Benson shot one of the family portraits, look!'

I pointed to one of the dark oil paintings hanging to the left of the fireplace. Sir Peregrine looked across to where I was pointing and gave a loud guffaw of laughter,

'Good God, young Ponsonby, you're quite right. Old Grandpops has been shot in the heart. Well, you said you were an art expert, what do you think? Ruined, what?'

I walked closer to the portrait and saw the neat hole surrounded by a burn mark and said,

'Oh dear, yes, but easily restored, Sir Peregrine. I know someone who could…

Sir Peregrine interrupted me, 'What a hoot you are, young Ponsonby. Talking art restoration at a time like this.' He gave another roar of laughter and added, 'You saved me from being shot, what's that? Better Grandpops being holed in my place. Always hated that old painting, what, a nasty greedy look in his eye as he looks down at one, don't you know.'

Our conversation about the art work was interrupted by Henry who was standing with one foot resting on Benson's chest. 'If you two have quite finished discussing the merits of the portrait could you tell me what was going on here?'

Sir Peregrine rose unsteadily from his chair and went over to look down at Benson who was now stirring and rubbing the back of his neck.

'Quite right, young man, explanations needed, what? Benson, here, went over the mark, pointed a pistol at me, Girlie's little lady's pistol, I believe. Rudely demanded the key to my secret cupboard.' He patted his jacket pocket and added, 'Always keep it on me, what's that, but, of course, Benson knows the cupboard and the jewels kept there, what? Family stuff, what, and the cupboards not very secret, just in a panel in my bedroom, don't you know?'

'And the coat-hanger?' Henry asked as he kicked aside the coat-hanger that was lying on the carpet beside Benson. 'Please don't tell me you attacked an armed man with a coat-hanger, Allie?'

I nodded and Rosso stood close beside me and nudged my hand. I was about to explain further when Benson sat up and a silver salver slipped out from under his jacket. It rolled across the carpet, span around a few times then lay flat. Henry quickly picked it up and running is fingers over the fluted edge, said.

'George the Third, lovely piece.'

There was another loud guffaw of laughter from Sir Peregrine and he said,

'Good God, I can see why you two are a good match, what's that. Young Ponsonby talking art restoration and the handsome Eye-tie dating the silver while the criminal comes around, what's that? Even I can see it's a bit eccentric, what?'

I wasn't sure whether to laugh with Sir Peregrine or to protest but there was no need for either. Suddenly we all looked to the window as the yellow light of a taxi shone in the darkness.

Chapter 28

"Painting is with me but another word for feeling."
John Constable

'Can't we just leave?' I muttered to Henry as we stood each side of Sir Peregrine in his wing chair. Benson was sitting on the carpet rubbing his head and Lady Agatha and Jasper were standing in the doorway, their hands and wrists bandaged, looking somewhat belligerent.

'How can we leave Sir Peregrine with this lot?' Henry muttered back and I sighed and knew he was right. Rosso was leaning into me but his long head was alert and his ears folded back. There was a long moment of complete silence and then Henry spoke aloud.

'Well, Sir Peregrine, just tell me what you would like me to do with this bunch of thieves.'

Jasper took a step forward and said, 'We only took what we deserve, we have a right…'

Henry took a step forward, too, and interrupted Jasper,

'I suggest you don't continue in that vein, Jasper. I owe you a punch on the nose and if your hands weren't bandaged I'd have delivered it by now. I asked Sir Peregrine, head of the family, what he would like me to do with you. For example, I could call the police.'

Benson struggled to his feet and wobbled over to pick up the silver salver and then sat down heavily on the carpet again as he said,

'No police, sir, I beg you. It was them two who led me along and I needed the money. I just want to go to my sister's in Abergavenny.'

'Abergavenny, what ho?' Sir Peregrine suddenly entered the conversation, 'Went there years ago… sounds like an eminently suitable plan, Benson. Why don't you keep the silver salver, George the whatever, and bugger off?

Henry and I exchanged glances of amazement and I said,

'But Sir Peregrine, Benson….'

'Yes, yes, I know what you're thinking, what's that, but I can't be dashed with the local bobbies all over the place. Bugger off, Benson before I'm persuaded to change my mind.'

Benson struggled once more to his feet, clutching the silver salver to his chest and stumbled toward the door. Lady Agatha and Jasper were standing in his way and Benson halted in front of them,

'You were never going to give me my share, were you?' Benson's voice was quiet but he carried on determinedly, 'I should never have listened to either of you. Sir Perry is a fine man and he's just proved it to me. You two deserve each other.'

Jasper raised a bandaged hand and said,

'You worthless little rat I could…'

Benson suddenly dodged between Lady Agatha and Jasper,

'But you can't, can you? Can't do much bullying with your hands like that. I'm off!' He sneered back at them as he went through the doorway and disappeared into the hall.

Henry moved forward and said, 'Shall I see him off the premises, Sir Peregrine?'

'No, no, dear chap, I have a feeling you had better stay here, what? The Labs can see Benson off.' Sir Peregrine chuckled and he gave a low whistle and the two Labs lurched to their feet and galloped out of the room. Rosso looked up at me and I stroked his head and said,

'We need you here, Rosso, stay with us. You can see your friends later.'

Rosso sat down on my foot but his ears were still laid back on his head and there was a raised line of hackles along his back. Sir Peregrine clapped his hands and said cheerily,

'When thieves fall out, what? Never thought I'd have a chance to see it in action, what's that? How does it go? When thieves fall out, honest men something or other, what's that?'

'I believe,' Henry said in an icy cold voice as he glared at Jasper, 'it's an old 16th century proverb, when thieves fall out, honest men come by their own.'

'That's it, that's it. Old Nanny used to say it, remember when you stole bits and pieces like that tin of biscuits, Jas?'

There was another long moment of silence, more awkward than before as we all, apart from Sir Peregrine, tried to decide on the next move. Sir

Peregrine seemed oblivious to the problem and broke the silence with a loud splutter of laughter,

'Fine state of affairs, what? You took it a bit far this time, Jaz old chap and you Girlie, you don't have much to say for yourself. Sorry your hands are hurt, what?'

Lady Agatha began to weep rather noisily and I thought Jasper would put his arm, bandaged as it was, around her but he just stood straight and still and ignored her.

"Poor old Girlie,' Sir Peregrine said, 'All a bit much, what? Why don't you and Jaz go down to the dower house and put up there for the night. I know you have your little love nest set up there.'

This seemed to shock Jasper and his shoulders drooped as he said,

'You knew about me and Aggie? How long have you known?'

'It's been a while, what's that? Knew the Women's Institute was all an excuse. Quite a while, yes, but then, you see, I have my Florrie.'

As though on cue at the sound of her name, a buxom blonde-haired woman burst through the door and said,

'What's up, Perry, my heart, you all right? What's a-happening?'

Chapter 29

"Fools talk of imitation and copying, all is imitation."
                              Thomas Gainsborough

I drove slowly down the icy pot-holed drive and away from Farley Hall. Whether it was the exhilaration of actually escaping or some form of mild hysteria but I began to laugh. I managed to go through the huge rusty gates and turn left but soon had to pull into a lay-by as my laughter made me too weak to continue. Henry was laughing, too, probably more at the helpless state that I was in than anything more. Rosso put his paws on my shoulders and pushed his long nose between us, looking from one to the other. I reached up and stroked his head and said,

'Oh, Rosso, it's all much too much!'

Rosso licked his lips and then yawned and turned away and curled up on the back seat.

'I agree, Rosso, it's a shame but the beautiful young woman has finally lost it.' Henry said still laughing, 'Shall I drive, my love?'

I nodded feebly and stepped out of the car and went around the bonnet. Henry held open the passenger door for me and suddenly another wave of laughter engulfed me and I doubled up, holding my ribs and tried to say,

'This is…this is… this is the very lay-by where it all started.'

Henry turned and looked into the ditch and said,

'You're right. There's where Sir Peregrine fell through the hedge. So you haven't completely lost your mind then, what's that?'

'Oh don't don't, Henry. I'll be sick if I laugh any more.'

'Get in the car, then. Come on, chop chop! We might get shot at any moment, what ho?'

This did nothing to stop my laughter but Henry bundled me into the passenger seat and went around to the driver's seat and quickly pulled away. The back wheels slid alarmingly and I clutched the side handle but Henry seemed unconcerned and just carried on, straightening the car and speeding onwards. At least the fright had stopped my fit of laughter and I was left with a bad case of hiccoughs.

'Don't drive so hicc fast, Hen- hicc - ry.'

'Just tighten your seat belt… this is nothing compared to the rally I won in the Basses-Alps. You forget how lucky you are to be driven by such an amazing driver.'

'Believe me, hicc Henry, I never forget you are a hicc racing driver.'

'Do you want some water? There's a flask of Perrier in the glove box.'

'How is it you always, always have everything I need hicc Henry?'

'I was put on this earth to serve you, I know that now, my heart!'

'Oh, don't, you'll start me off again. Wasn't it wonderful when Florrie burst in and hicc called Sir Perry 'my heart'?

'I think it's a very lovely term of endearment and I shall adopt it for you, my heart.'

'Please don't, I think you need a Norfolk accent to hicc get away with it.

'Maybe you're right, but it seems a shame. Perhaps I shall call you Girlie?'

'You just dare and I'll pour the rest of this delicious cold water over your immaculate tweed jacket.'

'You've already ruined one of my jackets sliding down that roof and cut a hole in my trousers, so please leave this one alone.'

'OK, but you have to admit I was incredibly brave out on that roof, wasn't I?'

'You were incredibly foolhardy and I can't bear to think about it. I'm scarred for life.'

'No you're not, just your Cashmere jacket is a bit scarred. Anyway, we'd still be in that horrid cold attic if I hadn't rescued us.'

'Horribly true. That doesn't bear thinking about either. I suppose the Labs and Florrie would have found us eventually.'

'I do think you're being slightly ungrateful and I may have to sprinkle a little cold water on your smooth back hair.'

I reached out and threatened to do so and Rosso stood up on the back seat and eyed me severely.

'It's OK, Rosso, I'm only joking. I know Henry's driving and at this speed he should concentrate. I just feel so elated to get away from the Hall. There's even a glimmer of wintry sunshine and we're going to the seaside.'

Rosso curled up again and I sat back quietly and drank the rest of the water.

'Far be it from me to dampen your spirits, my love,' said Henry glancing at me and smiling, 'and I'm as relieved as you are to get away. If I put my foot down we should make Holkham in time for a decent mid-morning coffee.'

'Your foot is already flat down, Henry, I'm sure it must be. But a good coffee is what I need. Sir Peregrine may love his Florrie dearly but I don't know how he survives her cooking.'

'Ghastly I agree, that bacon this morning, I was hungry but even I couldn't stomach it. She's the sort of cook that can burn boiling water. She's clever in other ways though.'

'True, she soon grasped the situation and proceeded to sort it out efficiently. I can see why she gets on well with Sir Peregrine.'

'In what way?' Henry turned to me and I closed my eyes as we side-slipped around a sharp bend in the narrow road.

'Can you at least look at the road as we skid along, please?' I opened my eyes and saw we had turned onto the coast road which at least was wider and had fewer bends. 'Well,' I added slowly as I thought about it, 'It's rather as though you think they're not even listening and then suddenly they go straight for the jugular. Like when Sir Peregrine said Jasper could keep the revenue from the tulip farm if they went to live in Holland…'

'Yes, I see what you mean. Florrie stepped in and said something about the apple orchard and some sort of a deal was clinched on the spot.'

'Exactly, there I was thinking about calling the police… after all they did try to steal the paintings and…'

'And knocked me out, drugged Sir Peregrine and trussed us both up… hard to forgive, I'd have thought.' Henry turned to me again, his dark eyebrows raised in question.'

'Eyes on the road, Henry, please. Although I do love your eyebrows.'

'My eyebrows? Is that all?'

'Hmm, no… there are other things about you, I suppose. Ah, there's a sign to Holkham, just two more miles to our hotel and I'll tell you in detail all the things I love about you.'

Rosso shuffled around on the back seat and gave a loud, exaggerated yawn.

Chapter 30

"Confound the nose, there's no end to it!"
Thomas Gainsborough

We had taken coffee in a glass-walled room that extended out to meet the North Sea. The wind blowing in from Siberia tossed the grey clouds around and it made the warmth of the room even more luxurious.

'I have to say that this place is even better than the pub I thought we'd go to, Henry. How did you find it?'

'I googled for the most expensive place to stay on the Norfolk coast and this popped up. I thought we deserved some luxury after the rigours of Farley Hall.'

'You do love throwing money around, don't you?' I stretched lazily and added, 'I can feel my muscles thawing out.'

'I've booked the spa for an hour or so and…'

'Spa? How glam Norfolk is becoming. Lovely idea, when did you manage to arrange all this?'

'I know you always think I never use my mobile but it comes in useful sometimes. I booked us in when I went to order a taxi for the singed lovers. What a pitiful sight they were. I've never hit a man with bandaged hands but I was sorely tempted when Jasper tried to justify the theft.'

'So arrogant.' I nodded, 'I hope old Sir Perry manages to stay in command of the situation.'

'I think Florrie will make sure he does. She's a formidable woman and I think her time has come.'

'True, I really think they are a good match, Perry and Florrie, it's almost ridiculous.'

'I liked what Sir Peregrine said about us being a good match… did he actually call us eccentric?'

I giggled at the thought and then a young woman, tall and elegant in a pale cream suit, arrived at our table.

'The spa is all yours, now sir, whenever you want. My name is Meadow and I'll be pleased to show you the way?'

I detected an Australian accent in the lilting up-speak of her voice. I put down my coffee and said,

'How lovely, yes, please do. Are you coming, Henry?'

'You go ahead, I'll give Rosso a run on the beach and join you.'

I patted both Henry and Rosso lightly on their heads and followed Meadow.

'Do you have a hotel shop, Meadow? I didn't know we were going to swim, so I don't have a costume.'

'Certainly, Madame, there's a small selection in the boutique just at the entrance to the spa.' She turned to me, as she said, 'Your husband has booked the whole spa for two hours so… ' Meadow gave a knowing smile under her long strong nose, 'So, in fact you don't need to use a cozzie and there are plenty of robes.'

I was about to say that Henry was not my husband but I rather liked the sound of it, so I just said firmly,

'Oh, I definitely want to buy a costume.'

Meadow nodded but looked rather disappointed and I felt very English. She made it worse by saying,

'We've never had a guest book the whole spa before. I think it's so romantic.'

'Oh it is, I agree, Henry is very romantic.' I sighed and thought to myself that he was also a dreadful spendthrift. Then, we arrived at the entrance to the spa and I quickly chose a dark navy bikini, disappointing Meadow once more by refusing the shocking pink swimsuit with huge cutout sides.

'You sure, that's the one?' The up-speak inflection in her voice making it sound as though she found it hard to believe. I took the bikini from her and hurried through the plate glass doors and into the spa. In less than five minutes I was lounging on a tubular curved bed that bubbled under me. The water was soft and warm, gently perfumed with lavender and I let the water take the weight of my body. The spa pool was not very large but had a huge waterfall at one end and small bays where jets of water ebbed and flowed. Yes, I thought to myself, Henry was right, we deserved some luxury. I looked up at the high glass ceiling and watched the grey clouds racing across the sky in a way that Constable would have admired. I closed my eyes, determined not to think about anything to do with Farley Hall. Then, I heard Henry's voice,

'There you are! Whatever are you lying on?'

I opened my eyes and saw Henry standing up straight in the water and looking down at me.

'It's lovely, try it… the bubbles come through the tubes .'

'It looks like an instrument of torture. Like the bikini though.'

He slipped his forefinger under the strap of my top and pretended to admire the material.'

'Henry, you have to behave.'

'I absolutely do not,' He said, lowering himself down to lie beside me, 'Although, good or bad behaviour is actually subject to … well, I'm not sure what. You fudge my brain, Allie. But I do know that no-one else is around so…' He ran his finger into the waistband of my bikini bottom and pulled me toward him.

'I bet there are loads of cameras around and the Aussie girl is bound to be watching a screen somewhere.'

Henry exhaled and pushed himself off the rack and sank to the bottom of the pool and sat there blowing bubbles. I laughed and slipped off the chrome tubes and joined him. We looked at each other through the water as we sat on the tiled pool floor and then he took me in his arms as we floated to the surface. I looked at him and caught my breath as I realised how much I loved him.

Henry brushed my hair back from forehead and said,

'Steam room or sauna? I don't believe they have cameras in either.'

I nodded and said, 'Why not both?'

Chapter 31

"The sky is the source of light in Nature and it governs everything."
John Constable

'I think my legs have turned to warm jelly.' I said as I threw myself on the bed in our room, 'I'm more than relaxed, I'm sort of dissolving. The spa was a wonderful idea.'

'Good, I'm so glad. You needed to be warmed through and through. Farley Hall was bitterly cold, wasn't it?'

I was about to agree when my mobile rang and I saw it was my brother,

'Sam, how are you? We haven't spoken for days.'

I switched my phone on to loudspeaker so that Henry could listen in as Sam replied,

'You left early from home, Suzie and I missed saying goodbye. Did you have a good time in Norfolk?'

I stretched my eyes wide at Henry, warning him not to say too much about the truly awful time we had endured.

'Well…' I hesitated, trying to think of a reasonable version of our time at Farley Hall, 'It was bitterly cold and Sir Peregrine is… well, eccentric to say the least.'

'His daughter is Fenella, is that the one?'

'Yes, fancy you remembering, Sam.'

'I can't forget her, she thought she was madly in love with me when we were teenagers and used to turn up at all my rugby matches. Was she there?'

'No, anyway, all my friends were madly in love with you. It was very trying at the time.'

'Pa said you and Henry were going to size up some painting or other. Was it any good?'

'Well, it was all rather complicated so…' I couldn't think how to begin any explanation or account of what had happened. I added, 'Let's just say I shall never forgive Pa for sending us there.'

"Oh, no good then. You always hate being cold. Have you warmed up now?'

'Oh yes, we're staying at this new lush hotel on the coast. Fantastic views of the sea and the sky. We've been in the spa for hours.'

'Spa? In Norfolk, Good God, what is the world coming to?'

'Oh, it was heavenly, I've never been so hot and wet.'

Henry put his head in his hands at my words and I rushed on, 'The pool is fantastic with a huge rushing waterfall and glass walls looking over to the sea.'

'You sure you're not making all this up, Allie? It just doesn't sound like Norfolk at all.'

'I know, but Henry found it… it's only been open a month. You and Suzie must try it some time.'

'Will do, maybe there will be some cheap offers after Christmas.'

'Christmas?'

'Dear Lord, Allie, don't tell me you've forgotten it's Christmas in two weeks time? All this lovey-dovey with Henry is frying your brain.'

'No, no, of course I hadn't forgotten.' But I had, so I decided to swerve the conversation, 'And careful what you say about Henry and lovey-dovey, our call is on speakerphone and he's right here.'

'That's OK,' Sam said, laughing, 'Hi Henry, hear you've been freezing in Farley Hall. My sympathies, my sister is a miserable little monster when she's cold.'

Henry took the phone from me,

'Hello, Sam, good to hear from you. You could have warned me about Allie's seriously bad behaviour in cold conditions. You told me to look out for her temper when she's hungry but nothing about cold temperatures. She was a bit fizzy.'

'Fizzy,' I shouted, grabbing for the phone, 'Give me back my phone, Henry!'

Henry held it up above his head and I jumped for it but missed and Henry continued talking to Sam,

'Right now she's ready for lunch so I'd better go and organise a feast. Speak soon, Sam and love to Suzie. Ciao!'

Henry passed me the phone and dodged the cushion that I threw at him and smiled one of his best dental smiles. It was hard to be angry with a man who could grin like the Cheshire Cat.

'So, Christmas then, Sam. Do you and Suzie have plans?'

'Suzie's parents are off ski-ing so we're going to be in Newmarket... you two, too, surely?'

'It would be lovely. I haven't asked Henry yet and he may want to visit his mother.'

'I'm sure Ma would love her and her Italian guy to come, too. Let's try and arrange it. Must go now as I have a one to one training session in a few minutes.'

'Anyone interesting?'

'She's so interesting that I can't even tell you who she is... but think Royal.'

'Gosh, Sam, that's amazing. Better not be late, then or you might be spending Christmas in the Tower.'

'Quite possible, speak soon then, Sis, best love and look after yourself. I have the distinct feeling you haven't told me everything that went on at Farley.'

'Can't think what you mean.' I said as nonchalantly as I could. 'Off you go, now, be a good courtier.'

The line dropped and I stared at the blank screen for a moment, knowing that Sam had, in his brotherly way, guessed that it had been more than cold at Farley Hall. I sighed as I thought how horrified Sam would have been if he knew that I had been scrambling over icy roof-tops.

Henry who had disappeared into the small dressing-room off the side our bedroom emerged looking totally immaculate in a dark grey cashmere roll neck and tweed trousers that only an Italian tailor could have cut.

'How do you do it?' I asked, 'Your Vuitton luggage is like some magic box. Do you have an endless supply of cashmere?'

'No, but I need to the way you get through my clothes. I must see my tailor when we get back to London.'

'You could go tomorrow afternoon.' I said, feeling rather guilty about his ripped jacket even though it had saved my favourite cashmere cardigan.

Henry came over to me and rested his hands on my shoulders and said quietly,

'I was going to tell you after you'd had lunch but… well, I'm afraid, tomorrow we must go back to Farley Hall?'

Chapter 32

"What's the use of a great city having temptations if fellows don't yield to them?"
P.G.Wodehouse

And so it was that, much against my will and better judgement, we were driving through the frosty Norfolk lanes back to Farley Hall. I had given up remonstrating and pleading and now sat next to Henry as he drove the Alfa at his usual rate, skidding around bends and hurtling along the narrow roads.

'Henry,' I said, clutching the swinging leather strap that dangled down beside my head, 'I'm trying very hard not to sulk but could you at least drive a little slower? I mean, what's the hurry to get back to Farley Hall?'

'Slower?' Henry turned to look at me, his dark eyebrows raised in the usual perfect arrows pointing up to his smooth liquorice hairline. 'But I am driving slowly especially for you.'

I sighed, defeated by his handsome face looking at me so fondly. I closed my eyes and clung onto the strap and stretched out my other hand to the dashboard to steady myself as I said,

'I suppose Jasper was driving too fast as they made their getaway with the paintings. It's so icy on these country rolylanes. Do be careful.'

'I am being very careful, my love, don't worry. They must have had quite an accident for their car to catch fire. Imagine trying to open the boot. Madness!'

'Madness mixed with greed.' I replied, 'And to think they were only fakes anyway. What do you think will happen when they find that out? I still can't believe Sir Peregrine just let them stay on the estate. Couldn't they be vindictive?'

'With their hands bandaged up, I suppose there's not much they can do. Anyway, that's partly why I thought we should check everything out this morning.'

'Well, I'm fed up with telling you that it's not our business… I think Sir Peregrine should call in the police and that's that.'

'But you know he won't, don't you? He'd never turn in his own brother and his wife.'

'I can't see why not. They deserve it.'

'I'm sure you're right but I'm also sure he just won't do it. He's very old school and likes to do things his own way.'

'Oh, I give up on it all. Sir Peregrine is mad as a hatter and you're not much better. Anyway, here we are again at the rusty old gates so let's just get on with it…. whatever 'it' is.'

'I've told you over and over, Allie, I thought we should stand by Sir Peregrine while he sorts things out with Jasper. Shouldn't take long.' Henry swung the car through the gates and we bumped along the pot-holed drive up to the Hall. As we reached the front doors, Henry turned to me again and added, 'Sir Peregrine's asked us to go to the bank with him later.'

'To the bank? Where? Why didn't you tell me before?'

'Er, I forgot?'

'Henry di Palliano you are a dreadful liar. How can you say that you forgot?'

'Well, all right, not forgot exactly, but I thought I'd tell you later.'

'As if that would make it any better. I thought we'd be back in London by tonight.'

'Well, that's all right then,' Henry said cheerfully, 'Sir Peregrine's bank is in the Strand… I said we'd drive him up there.'

'This just gets better and better.' I was about to say more but at that moment, Henry turned off the silent engine and Sir Peregrine, accompanied by the two black Labradors, came stumbling down the steps to greet us. He came to my door and opened it,

'Good Morning, young Ponsonby, you're looking more beautiful than ever. Thank you so much for coming back here today. I'm sure there are many things you'd rather be doing, what's that?'

I stepped out of the car and I heard myself saying.

'Not at all, Sir Peregrine, it's our pleasure.'

Chapter 33

"I know I was writing stories when I was five. I don't know what I did before that. Just loafed, I suppose."

P.G.Wodehouse

'Best room in the whole place, what?' Sir Peregrine was sitting in a chair close to the Aga and drinking coffee, 'Sure you won't have coffee, you two lovebirds? Never tasted better than the coffee dear Florrie brews, what's that?'

I shook my head hastily but Henry said politely,

'Thank you, sir, but we took coffee earlier. We don't have much time if we're to get to London by three-thirty.'

'Ah yes, not good to be late for the bank johnnies, what, all such a very uptight lot. I've told them we want to take out the paintings and it caused a helluva fuss.'

'Well, sir, they are extremely valuable works of art. I expect there's a good deal of insurance attached.' Henry sighed as Sir Peregrine was stroking one of his Labradors and seemed to have lost interest.

I decided to enter the conversation,

'You know, Sir Peregrine, the last Constable sold at Christie's for well over twenty-two million pounds. It was a record breaking price.'

Sir Peregrine carried on stroking his dog and said,

'Well, well, young Ponsonby, you know your stuff, what's that, but my Constable's only a muddy daub.'

'But if it's a genuine Constable then…'

Sir Peregrine looked up sharply and seemed to pay attention at last,

'If? What's that? It's genuine all right. The fake has burnt to cinders, don't you recall, young lady?'

I nodded feebly, deciding not to continue on that track and said,

'Have you seen Lady Agatha and Jasper yet today?'

Sir Peregrine gave one of his loud snorts of laughter,

'Not I, not I… but Florrie went down to the Dower House to see what's what and they've scarpered again. Taken the old Volvo estate this time, what.'

'Goodness!' My voice now sounded more feeble than before. 'Perhaps it's a … ' I searched for the right thing to say and failed. Sir Peregrine roared with laughter again and interrupted me,

'Perhaps it a good thing? What's that? Yes, young Ponsonby, I'd say it's a very good thing. Now, Florrie is going to move in here and be with me, what, couldn't be better, don't you know.'

For the second time in twenty-four hours, Florrie came onto the scene on cue. She entered the kitchen so abruptly that I wondered if she had been eavesdropping.

Sir Peregrine rose to his great height and went over to her,

'And here she is… always there when needed, what's that?' Sir Peregrine put his arm around Florrie's shoulders and said, 'We grew up together on the estate, what, Florrie here is the daughter of my old Nanny, what's that, and dear Nanny taught her how to cook.'

Henry and I exchanged quick glances, unnoticed by either Sir Peregrine or Florrie who were looking into each other's eyes and smiling. Sir Peregrine continued,

'We had such fine times playing together as children, I was always loafing around looking for her... but naturally, what, as we grew up, we fell in love.'

Florrie, her cheeks already rosy now blushed a deep scarlet as she said,

'But, a-course, it couldn't be, Perry was to be Lord of the place and I was just the daughter of an unmarried woman. My Ma had slipped up, you see when she was a very young woman and old Sir Jerome, Perry's father had taken pity on her and given her a place here so as she could keep me.'

Sir Peregrine patted her on the shoulder and said kindly,

'Nothing to stop us now, my dear, now we can be together at last, what. Poor Girlie never wanted to marry me, either, but that was how it was arranged then.'

Florrie brushed tears away from her eyes with her apron and said briskly,

'I'd best get on with an early lunch if you going up to the London, Perry. Would you fancy my macaroni cheese?'

'Would I indeed, what?' Sir Peregrine beamed with delight and then said, 'You two lovebirds have no idea how delicious it is.'

I spoke hastily,

'Don't worry about us, please, we've had the most enormous breakfast.'

Henry followed quickly with the same,

'Another time, perhaps, but right now I think Allie and I should get on with valuing… maybe we could go back to the attic and make some sort of inventory of anything you might want to sell?'

'Sell?' Sir Peregrine repeated vaguely, 'Oh, indeed, do as you wish. I'm not at all interested in the old relics up there. Load of rubbish and broken furniture, what's that?'

Florrie who was grating cheese, turned around from the worktop and said in a firm voice,

'Now, now, Perry, my heart, you should be glad these two clever young people have come to help you. You need to sell a mighty number of things to pay for the renovations. Don't want Farley Hall to crumble down on your watch, do you? And, what's more, we need money for all the plans I have in mind. Planting barley in the sandy fields down to the sea… shame that land's been let lie fallow. I have a hundred ideas and more.'

'Isn't she a wonder, what?' Sir Peregrine returned to the chair by the fire and added, 'You know I've been in love with her as long as I can recall, what? By the time I was five years old I couldn't do without her, don't you know. My Florrie will see to things, what's that, yes, yes, I'd be very grateful if you two clever lovebirds would have a look-see… go anywhere you want, have a recce before we leave for London, much obliged, what's that.'

'That's right, Perry, my heart, now you rest up awhile, you've got a long day ahead.

There was hardly need for her to speak as Sir Peregrine was already fast asleep and snoring gently.

Chapter 34

"It is true of course, that I have a will of iron, but it can be switched off if the circumstances seem to demand it."

P.G.Wodehouse

'I can't believe we came back here, let alone up in this miserable cold attic.' I kicked grumpily at a pile of crumpled newspapers that lay beside a crate.'

'You can go back down to the kitchen if you want, my love.' Henry was holding a very large torch and flashing it around the rafters, 'I'm going to go through this attic at least but there may be more.'

'Oh God, that's a dreadful thought.' I turned on the torch that Henry had given me and pointed it at the old leather trunk under the gap in the roof. 'No, I'll stay with you. I suppose it is our work and this place could be plum-full of treasures.'

'That's the spirit, my love. I'm surprised Rosso decided to stay by the Aga with his Labrador friends. What a turncoat!'

'Oh, I don't blame him at all. It's not often he has a chance to make friends and I'm sure Florrie will give him some titbits.'

'Rather him than me… her cooking really is dreadful.'

'Well, at least Sir Peregrine likes it.'

'Unbelievable what love can do to a man.'

'Or a woman. I mean if somebody told me this time last year that I'd be in a dark old attic hunting for relics and treasures I should never have believed it possible. But here I am!'

'So you do love me a little then?'

'No, I love you lots and lots but this is not the time or place, Henry, definitely not.'

Henry had come over to where I was standing by the trunk and put his arms around me. He sighed and said,

'You're right, of course, so let's get started. I'll go through the trunk of mouldy old clothes and you take photos of all the broken furniture. Is that a good idea?'

Henry had a charming way of giving an order and at the same time asking if the person involved wanted to do it. Somehow, there was never any option to refuse… he asked so politely. In fact, I thought it to be a good option as I hated musty old clothes. I began to move around the sides of the room, shining the torch and taking photos of broken chairs and tables. There was no doubt at all that the Palliano workshop would be very busy. There were no less that five broken Chinese Chippendale dining chairs thrown under the eaves and two Hepplewhite chairs that matched the one in our bedroom. I began to warm up as I worked, feeling the rising excitement of discovery. I was about to move a dustcover off a large piece of furniture when Henry suddenly called out,

'Allie, oh my God, Allie look at this!'

I dropped the dust sheet and went over to where Henry was standing, shining his torch onto a large piece of jewellery almost as big as his hand.

'What is it? Some sort of brooch?'

Before Henry could answer a girl's voice called out my name,

'Alicia, Alicia, where are you? Allie, where are you?'

I went over to the door and came face to face with Fenella Jerome, my old schoolfriend and tennis partner.

'Fenella, what are you doing here? I said, staring at her face which was at the same time very familiar and yet changed.

'Allie, good to see you, have you forgotten I live in this old pile of timber and stone. More to the point, what are you doing here?'

I stepped back and she came into the attic and then stopped,

'Oh, sorry, I didn't realise you were with someone. What's going on? Pa was sound asleep in the kitchen and Florrie was standing at the Aga with the Labradors and some huge wild looking dog that I've never seen the like of... now I find you up in this dreadful attic with a man who looks like a movie star. Florrie said I'd find you in an attic but... well, it's all very strange.'

Henry came forward and held out his hand to Fenella.

'Henry di Palliano, pleased to meet you. Allie and I are here to value some of your father's antiques. I'm sorry if we alarmed you.'

'Alarmed me? No, not at all, taken my breath away, maybe? Pleased to meet you.' Fenella had taken

Henry's hand and was holding on to it for far too long.

'Henry's my boyfriend and my boss, Fenella.' I said firmly and gave her a light nudge in the ribs. She dropped Henry's hand and laughed,

'I see!' She said, 'What a damned shame. You Henry di Pally whoever are the most interesting thing I've seen around this old place for a very long time. Not that I'm surprised, Allie always wins the prize, always did. At school she was always top at everything and so sweet that we couldn't even hate her.'

I shook my head in embarrassment as Fenella continued to tease me and I noticed that Henry, while giving Fenella full benefit of his most charming smile, had slipped the large brooch into his pocket. When Fenella finally slowed down, Henry said,

'We've found a trunk of clothes, neither of us are experts in that field but Allie has a friend at the V & A who we think would be very interested to see them. Do you know anything about them?' Henry held the hat over his head and raised his eyebrows at Fenella.

'Oh, that's old Nelson's stuff. We used to play with it when I had friends to stay. I believe my grandfather was a fanatic collector of Nelson memorabilia. Of course, you know Nelson was born in the village here. Our local hero. I remember my mother saying something about Grandpops wasting a fortune on buying something of Nelson's, but I was too young to understand. The whole family are good at squandering money. It's a genetic trait! Fenella laughed, a more feminine version of Sir Peregrine's guffaw and Henry nodded, seeming to be thinking of something else. I took over the conversation,

'Your mother also mentioned that somewhere or other there was a box, a sort of light box with pictures? Do you know anything about it?'

'Oh yeh,' Fenella drawled, 'I know what you mean, an old sort of magic lantern, but it wasn't much fun. I thought it was going to be naughty pictures but it was just landscapes and that sort of thing. It used to be in a tea-chest over there.' She wandered over to the far end of the attic and I followed her with my torch. She pushed aside a few dusty cardboard boxes and said,

'Yes, it's still here. Is this what you meant?' She shoved the tea-chest to me with her foot and I held my breath as I carefully opened it and saw a large dark box inside, so similar to the one I had seen at the V & A… it was almost certainly one of Gainsborough's show-boxes of paintings on glass. Henry had come over to stand beside us and he looked up at the gaping hole in the rafters and said quietly,

'I think the problem of repairing the roofs is solved.'

Chapter 35

"I am Psmith," said the old Etonian reverently. "There is a preliminary P before the name. This, however, is silent. Like the tomb. Compare such words as ptarmigan, psalm, and phthisis."

P.G.Wodehouse

The Alfa was packed to the gunnels as we drove away from Farley Hall. Florrie stood on the icy steps waving us farewell and Sir Peregrine had a tear in his eye as he waved back. He was sitting in the front passenger seat beside Henry, his head almost touching the velvety roof panel. There had been some discussion whether Henry or I should drive and Fenella had been very keen, too keen, to sit in the back with Henry and Rosso. Henry had quickly declared that he would prefer to drive on the icy roads and take the responsibility for the precious cargo. Normally I would have objected but, for once, I just agreed and said sweetly,

'It's true, Henry, my love, you have so much more experience of driving in wintry conditions… all that rally driving in the Alps. I shall squash in the back with Fenella and Rosso.'

Rosso had been having a final chase around the rose gardens with his Labrador friends but, at my words, he had jumped into the back and curled up on the floor. Now, as Henry swung the car through the gates, Rosso yawned and rested one paw and his head on my knee.

I stroked smooth the feathery hairs on his forehead and said,

'You will miss the Labs, won't you.'

Sir Peregrine said,

'Indeed, but I shall soon be back, what's that?'

Fenella and I exchanged smiles and began to giggle like two schoolgirls.

'Oh Pa,' Fenella said, trying not to laugh aloud, 'Allie meant Rosso would miss the Labs, not you.'

'What's that? Now don't be silly, Fenella, what. Let's just enjoy the journey. Such a car, Henry, and all electric, what? How long does she run for?'

Henry and Sir Peregrine entered a long conversation about the joys of the Alfa Pininfarina and Fenella and I began to chat quietly,

'Do you really think all the junk in the boot is worth something?' Fenella asked.

'Oh goodness, yes, a small fortune. If your father decides to sell, then the family shouldn't have any money worries for a long time.'

'Oh, I'm sure he'll sell any of it. Pa doesn't care about such stuff…especially now he has Florrie installed at the Hall.'

I cast a sideways glance at Fenella, wondering if the idea disturbed her and I hesitated to reply but she carried on happily,

'It's all such a relief that it's out in the open. My Ma and Uncle Jaz have been an item for as long as I was old enough to understand. As for Florrie, she's a darling and always looked after me like a real mother. I mean, I love Ma, of course, but she can be very vague and distant. I think she'll be so much happier living in Holland.'

'I see,' I said untruly as I was finding it hard to keep up and wondering how much Fenella knew about the absconding pair and the theft of the paintings. Fenella carried on,

'Yes, Ma and Jaz will be so much happier there. I went to stay on our tulip farm one Easter hols. The manor house is lovely and surrounded by tulip fields, not to mention they'll like the easy supply of dope.'

'Dope!' I repeated the word in surprise and Fenella laughed,

'Oh, hadn't you noticed? Ma and Uncle Jaz are utter dope-heads. Nothing too nasty, just weed... I suppose they were hippies once.'

'Hmm,' I managed to mumble, trying to sound as though I agreed and thinking about my own parents, always so straight and dependable.

'Yes, they'll be so happy in Holland, floating around the tulip fields!' Fenella gave one of her inherited snorting laughs and I said,

'So you're happy with it all, I'm so glad.'

'Why on earth shouldn't I be? Anyway, I only came down to tell the ageing parents and fond uncle that I'm off to live in Shanghai.'

'Shanghai?' I realised I had fallen into stupid one word repetitions, so I tried harder and added, 'Do you have a job there?'

'Yeh, an offer I couldn't refuse from an IT company.'

I was about to repeat 'IT' but managed to stop myself in time and stayed silent. Fenella carried on,

'Yeh, the guy I'm living with is coming with me. He has to find a job there but I'll sort out something.' Fenella looked out the window as though she could already see the towering skyline of the Pearl of Asia. Then with a small sigh of satisfaction, she turned back to me and said, 'So what's all this about valuing art and old stuff?'

'Well, I left the auction house to work for Palliano's and now I travel with Henry, sourcing antiques and works of art for private collectors.'

'Palliano's... I've heard of them, classy Mayfair joint, isn't it? Good God, sounds like a dream job, Allie, but you always did go off with the first prize.' She laughed again, more of a snigger than a guffaw, and added, 'Are you...' She nodded her head in Henry's direction, 'Are you sleeping with Prince P for Palliano Charming then?'

I nodded and smirked and felt the colour rush to my cheeks but said nothing. Fenella raised her eyebrows and said,

'Definitely first prize material, I'd say.' She lowered her voice and said, 'Is he good in the sack?'

I drew in my breath and hastily turned to stroking Rosso's head and Fenella threw back her head and gave a loud Jerome roar of laughter. So loud that Sir Peregrine turned around a little and said,

'What are you up to, Fenella? What's that, behave yourself.'

'Oh Pa, we were just chatting about the precious booty in the car.'

She laughed again and then said,

'But seriously, Allie, do you really think that old light-box thing is valuable… and all those mouldy old clothes?'

I nodded and stayed silent as I turned to look out the side window at the frosty Norfolk fields.

Chapter 36

"What do ties matter, Jeeves, at a time like this?'
There is no time, sir, at which ties do not matter."
                                                P.G.Wodehouse

'Hey, Henry!' Fenella leaned across me and Rosso to tap Henry on the shoulder. 'Could you pull over and drop me off here?'

I looked out of the window and saw we had just turned into Millbank and were running along the river. I looked at Fenella in amazement and said,

'But aren't you coming to the bank? I thought you'd want to stay with your father and see…'

'See what, Allie? Nothing I haven't seen before and been bored to tears with… that old dark landscape or something? Good Lord, no way.' She raised her eyes to the ceiling as if to indicate I was mad and then tapped her father on the shoulder as Henry pulled into the lay-by outside the Tate. 'Pa? Are you awake? I'm off now. Lots of love and all that, good luck with everything.'

Sir Peregrine may have been asleep but he rallied quickly and said,

'Good luck to you, too, my dear little Girlie, new job, what's that?'

'Yes, Pa, as I told you.' She gave me a small grimace and then Sir Peregrine said,

'Shanghai, what, I have a few old muckers living out there. Let me know if you need any contacts, what's that?'

Fenella smiled in delight and tapped the top of Sir Peregrine's bald head.

'So you were listening, Pa, I thought…'

'Never mind what you thought, little Girlie , jump out now before Henry gets booked. We're blocking an ice cream van now. You know what they can be like, the ice cream Mafia.'

'I'll let you know my address as soon as I have a fixed abode, Pa…' She turned quickly to me, 'You, too, Allie, we must keep in touch. Let me know any time you're in Shanghai… and you Henry'… let me know if you get fed up with clever little Allie any time.'

I exchanged a quick glance with Henry in the driving mirror and he smiled at me as I said,

'Honestly, Fenella, you haven't changed much.'

'Don't intend to either, Als, I like me just as I am. Thanks so much for the lift, I would have suffered the awful train otherwise. I've been banned from driving for a few months but what the hell, it'll all be taxis and chauffeured limos in Shanghai.'

She suddenly leaned forward and hugged me and then stroked Rosso,

'It's been great seeing you again, Allie, remember me to your bro… tell him any time he's in Shanghai… oh, there's a taxi dropping off some tourists. I'll catch it! Bye!'

I watched as she hurled herself through a group of Japanese tourists and stopped the taxi driver. Henry suddenly jumped out of the car and said

'Her bag, it's in the boot. Fenella!' Henry dashed to the boot and pulled out Fenella's large tote bag and ran to the taxi as Fenella was about to jump in. She turned and saw Henry and, as he handed her the bag, she threw her arms around his neck and kissed him on both cheeks. Then she waved to me in the Alfa and shrugged. As the taxi drew away and Henry ran back to the Alfa, I realised that the Jeromes had quite a way of being thoroughly annoying and completely endearing at the same time.

Henry began to pull away just as a policeman was walking towards us and he wound down his window and said,

'Sorry, officer, I realise I am completely in the wrong but I was trying to handle a very difficult young woman.'

To my surprise the policeman raised his hand to his helmet and laughed,

'Quite all right, sir, we're just a bit hot on security here.'

'Absolutely, I quite understand and you're doing a great job at keeping us all safe in London. I'll get out of the way immediately.'

The policeman touched his helmet again in a small salute and then raised his arm to stop a line of taxis arriving and beckoned Henry through.

I sat back and said to Rosso,

'It's not just the Jeromes who charm their way through the world, Rosso, is it?

Rosso moved up on the seat in the space that Fenella had left and yawned then licked his lips.

'Are you worried about something, Rosso or just missing your Labrador friends?'

Rosso made no answer unless turning his back on me could be called such. I stroked his back and said,

'I'm sure it will all be fine now, don't worry. We're nearly at the bank now. I sat forward, stretching my seat belt, I put my head between Sir Peregrine and Henry and said,

'It's in the Strand, you said, didn't you? Nearly there then. I'm so excited to see the painting.'

Sir Peregrine reached up and patted my head, 'It's not much good, don't you know, all clouds and a muddy river, what. If you two think it's worth anything I'm happy to sell it. Florrie thinks so, too, and she has so may plans for dragging the old pile into the 21st century, what's that… talk of shooting parties and something about wedding venues. My Florrie has always been brim full of ideas, what.'

'Fingers crossed then, Sir Peregrine,' I said, sitting back again and hoping that we hadn't raised his hopes of saving Farley Hall only to find out the painting really was a muddy daub and not a Constable.

We rolled up outside Coutts impressive high glass walls and, rather to my dismay, Henry pulled onto the wide pavement. Two armed security guards immediately moved toward us but were stopped by a young man in impressive dark maroon livery. He wore a long coat with as many shiny buttons as Nelson's great-coat and a very neat navy blue tie, shiny black shoes and, best of all, a welcome smile.

'Count di Palliano, you made good time, sir.'

Henry jumped out of the Alfa and opened my back door as the young man opened the front passenger door for Sir Peregrine.

'Thank you, James,' Henry clapped the young man on the back and at the same time I noticed he slipped a wad of notes into the maroon braided pocket. Then he said, 'Make sure you plug her in. We've had quite a long run from Norfolk.'

'Certainly, sir, of course, leave it to me.'

Henry tossed him the keys and came over to me and put his arm around my shoulders ,

'Right, this is it then.'

I looked at Henry and whispered, 'Do you think it's OK to leave all that stuff in the boot?'

Henry smiled and shrugged, 'Well, if you can't trust Coutts, then who can you trust. I've arranged for Securicor to collect everything in an hour. We'll look at the Constable first and then…'

Sir Peregrine who was just entering the bank turned and said,

'And the Gainsborough, what's that, now that's a pretty picture, not so sure I want to sell it but see what you think, what. Come on, young Ponsonby, time to do your stuff.'

I followed Sir Peregrine into the foyer and suddenly felt aware that I was wearing muddy boots and Henry's Barber jacket. I glanced at Sir Peregrine and saw he was still wearing his slippers and a battered tweed suit. Henry, of course, was immaculately dressed in a dark business suit, how, I really didn't know. He moved ahead of us with Rosso at his side and was immediately the centre of attention.

Chapter 37

"One part of a picture ought to be like the first part of a tune; that you can guess what follows, and that makes the second part of the tune and so I've done."
Thomas Gainsborough

Inside a bank vault was not at all as I had imagined. After Sir Peregrine has signed, or rather dragged a pen across a few forms we had been escorted by two more uniformed men to a small escalator behind the main one that rose up from the foyer. We descended in steely, glassy silence, Henry carrying Rosso in his arms, and I began to feel slightly claustrophobic. I wanted so much to see the paintings that I took a deep breath and tried to relax my shoulders. Henry, on the step behind me, managed to pat his hand on my shoulder and Rosso reached out a paw and did the same. I stared down at my muddy boots and caught a glimpse of Sir Peregrine's slippers on the step below me and tried not to giggle, thinking how very odd we must all look. To my relief, as we reached the lower floor we were ushered into a room, more like a hotel lounge than a vault although there were noticeably no windows.

Sir Peregrine strode into the middle of the room said loudly,

'Jolly good, chaps, all nicely arranged but we need some coffee and a few bikkies, what's that?'

The older of the two escorts looked a little alarmed and then said quickly,

'Certainly, sir, of course sir, right away.' He spoke into his mouthpiece and I noticed his uniform and that of his colleague included a gun belt and a neat black gun in a holster. Henry gave me a gentle nudge in the middle of my back and I realised I had been frozen to the spot and gawping. I moved forward and Rosso kept close beside me as we crossed the marble floor. I sat on a leather sofa opposite to Sir Peregrine who had lowered himself gingerly into a low armchair and Rosso laid down across my feet. Between us was a chrome rack on wheels with two neat canvas bags obviously holding the paintings. I stared at them in excited anticipation and then Henry said,

'Shall I do the honours, sir?' He rested his hand on the strap of the smaller bag and looked at Sir Peregrine and waited.

'Go ahead, dear boy, do what you want, what's that. Bit of a fuss, isn't it about a couple of pictures that have been hanging around the place for as long as I can recall? Open up, what's that, by all means.'

He turned to the two guards who were standing each side of the door and shouted, 'Where's the coffee and bikkies? I used to come down here with my father and I always had a biscuit, chocolate, too.'

Henry laughed and said, 'It's strange you should say that as it is one of the few memories I have of being with my own father. He brought me down here…' Henry looked around, 'Modernised now, of course.'

I looked at Henry in surprise, my fixed stare momentarily drawn away from the canvas bags. Henry so seldom talked about his father and I had no idea that the Pallianos had an account here. It didn't seem the right time to ask him to tell more and anyway, at that moment there was an electronic buzz and one of the guards opened the door and took a tray from someone outside. He carried it to the glass coffee table beside Sir Peregrine, looking uncomfortable in the role of a waiter.

Sir Peregrine, however, was delighted and said,

'Jolly good, well done, young man, leave it there. I'll manage, what?'

The guard left the tray and stepped backward to the door and Sir Peregrine passed me the plate of biscuits.

'Take two, young Ponsonby, you look a bit peaky, what's that. Long journey up here and anyway, don't you know, you're all skin and bones, need fattening up, what's that?'

I took a biscuit and nodded, my voice seemed to have been left on the floor above somewhere and slowly unwrapped the biscuit and nibbled it.

Sir Peregrine, on the contrary was in full voice as he carried on,

'That's the ticket, nothing like a bit of chocolate to cheer you up, what?' He unwrapped another and lobbed it over to Rosso who snapped it up adroitly and crunched it quickly with one eye on Henry.

Henry wasn't even looking at Rosso as he had opened the first bag and had drawn out a gilt framed painting and was holding it in front of him.

I drew in my breath sharply and stood up, still holding half the biscuit and peered at the painting. It was a delightful landscape and yes, I found myself nodding, quite possibly a genuine Gainsborough.

Henry held the heavy ormolu frame lightly and turned to place it on a small easel that stood between the sofas.

'What do you think, Allie?' He took a step back and I joined him and we both gazed at the painting in silence. Sir Peregrine spoke up,

'That's the one I like, what, not bad is it. A few trees and the cows sloshing about in the shallows of a river, what's that? Not bad, is it?'

I knew that I should say something but my mouth seemed too full of chocolate biscuit. I swallowed hard and then felt Rosso at my side, conveniently taking the rest of the biscuit from my hand. I peered closer at the painting and then brought out a magnifying glass from my bag. The amber colour of the loose brush strokes in the trees showed under the strong magnification, bold and flowing, the precursor of all the impressionists that would follow. I stepped back to enjoy the effect from the correct distance to view the painting and the trees almost moved in the breeze. I turned to Sir Peregrine,

'It's a beautiful painting. I can quite see why you love it.'

'Love it? What's that? That's a bit strong, young Ponsonby, don't you know, but I can see it's pretty.'

I looked at Henry and he raised his eyebrows but I didn't want to make any definite decision, so I said cautiously,

'I think the National would be very interested in seeing it.'

I moved forward again and held the magnifying glass over the signature. Thos Gainsborough showed clearly enough through the grimy varnish but I was very aware of historic cases of forgery. I had researched enough to know that under close inspection of the signature there had been pencil lines showing around the letters. The signature had been fake and the work not authenticated. Although my instinct told me this lovely Suffolk landscape, a scene that I felt I knew from the fields around my home… surely was the work of Gainsborough? I stepped back again and said quietly,

'It feels so right but it should undergo rigorous forensic inspection… pigment and fibre sampling and date identification. It should go to the National Gallery first and foremost and they will advise further and recommend a specialist scholar to…'

Sir Peregrine interrupted me,

'Poppycock, can't be doing with all that rubbish, what? It's my Gainsborough and I'll take it home with me. I like it well enough, don't you know. Have another biscuit, young Ponsonby and don't look so worried, what?'

Henry took the painting off the easel and slid it carefully back into the canvas bag but said nothing. I shook my head at Sir Peregrine and his offer of another biscuit and said,

'Of course, it's completely up to you, Sir Peregrine.'

'Don't want to disappoint, dear girl, why don't you do some of your jiggery pokery lark on the Constable, what?

Henry carried the larger canvas bag over to the easel and slid the second painting carefully into view. He rested it on the ledge of the easel and then stood back. I joined him again and once more we fell silent. The painting had the magical power of a masterpiece and held us in its thrall. Once more Sir Peregrine broke the silence,

'That's the one, that's the muddy daub, what? Can't see anything for looking, what's that. Dreary, depressing piece of work if ever I saw one. Yes, do all you want testing that one, what, shouldn't mind at all selling the thing, don't you know?'

Chapter 38

"To find a man's true character, play golf with him."

P.G.Wodehouse

'If I were a betting man,' Henry said, nodding his head as he slipped his arm through mine. 'I'd lay a monkey on the Constable being genuine.'

'You are a betting man, Henry, I do believe you would lay a monkey on the last putt of an eighteen hole round of golf.'

Henry laughed and gave my arm a squeeze. We were standing in the rear entrance of the bank, waiting for the second Securior van to draw into place, the first having just pulled out of the car park on its way to the National Gallery.

'You may be right but I'm cautious by nature. I could so easily have driven the paintings around the corner in the Alfa but…well, and then there's the insurance and a deal of protocol now.'

'Not to mention the boot being full of the next cargo for the V & A.' I gave his arm a return squeeze and added, 'I don't think you are a cautious man, Henry, just very, very good at organisation. When and how did you plan this visit to the bank? I didn't even know you held an account here.'

Henry shrugged and said, 'Oh, I don't now... I think Ma still runs a checking account but we don't have a anything in the vaults. Long gone!'

'But you remember coming here with your father?'

'Hmm, I can only have been around five or six but I recall a few velvet bags of jewels. So, do you play golf, what's that?'

I realised that Henry was changing the subject and this was not the time to go back to his childhood, so I said,

'I certainly do. Sam and I went mad on the game when we were kids. One summer we played nearly every day on the course in Newmarket. It runs along the race track.'

'There's still so much I don't know about you, Allie.' My arm received another squeeze as he said, 'It's so wonderful that we have time, glorious years of time ahead of us. When the weather warms up a bit we must have a round... and with Sam.'

'Oh, Sam would play you with red balls in the snow. He's very good now... not sure he doesn't play off scratch. I wouldn't put one of your monkeys on beating him.'

Henry laughed, 'Then he'd have to give me five points.'

I was about to reply in surprise finding Henry had a handicap of five when I hadn't even know he played, but at that moment the second Securicor van drew up alongside the Alfa. Sir Peregrine wound down the passenger window and leaned out with Rosso's head poking over his shoulder,

'You two chatting away, what, time to get on, don't you know.'

'Certainly, sir,' Henry said, 'I wanted to wait for the van to draw up before opening the boot. Just a precaution.' He laughed and added, 'I'm a cautious type.'

'Doubt that, what's that, your Eyetie blood won't allow it. I'd put you down as a daredevil, what. Anyway, only a load of junk in the boot now, what's that.'

'Let's just get it all to the V & A and let the experts decide, Sir Peregrine.' I said as the two guards jumped out of the van and stood at the rear of the Alfa. Rosso swivelled his long neck around and gave a low growl. 'Behave, Rosso,' I said, stroking his head, 'We won't be long now.'

Henry opened the boot and the box containing the light-box and the suitcase of clothes were soon transferred into the van. The guards said nothing at all but jumped back into the van and started the engine.

'We may as well follow them.' Henry said, opening the back door and almost pushing me in next to Rosso. Then, he ran to the driver's seat and started the engine. I scrabbled for my seat belt as Henry savagely swung the Alfa around and followed the Securicor van out of the car park.

'Buckle up, everyone, it will be a fast drive through the traffic, faster if we stay behind the van.'

I sighed and Rosso settled down on the floor of the car and licked his lips nervously.

'You just love a car chase, don't you, Henry.' I said.

Sir Peregrine laughed and slapped his bony knee with one hand and held onto the leather strap with the other,

'Excellent, don't apologise, young man, that's the spirit, what, follow the van... race across London in the rush hour, what's that! Have the idea you are usually the one in front, though, Henry old chap. You eye-ties are the fast Johnnies on the race track, quick off the block, don't you know, what?'

Chapter 39

"There is only one cure for grey hair. It was invented by a Frenchman. It is called the guillotine."
P.G.Wodehouse

'Why the hell are they crossing the river at Vauxhall?' Henry tapped the steering wheel with impatience, 'I know the traffic is bad but it never works to cross to the South and back over again.'

'I'm sure they know what they're doing, Henry. Just try and keep up with them.'

Sir Peregrine gave a chortle of loud laughter,

'That's right, young Ponsonby, you tell him! As if the poor chap isn't slewing through the traffic fast enough, what's that!' He dissolved into more laughter and slapped his knee again in delight. I sat back, one hand resting on Rosso's head who was still sitting on the floor.

'No,' Henry seemed to be losing his usual calm control and in his turn slapped the steering wheel. 'He's heading too far south, the idiot.'

I leaned forward, stretching my seat belt and peered through the front windscreen at the rear of the Securicor van. Quite suddenly my stomach butterflied and I gripped the back of Henry's seat just as he said,

'Something's up. This is not right.'

'Where's he heading for?' I said, 'Are you sure the driver had the V & A as drop off address?'

'Absolutely certain, here, take my phone, Allie. You'll find the Securicor number in my recent calls, the last one. Would you ring them.'

Henry reached back with his mobile and I stabbed at the last call frantically.

'Only voicemail,' I said, 'How can that be?'

'Something is wrong, very wrong,' Henry spoke quietly now and at the same time aggressively overtook a taxi that had pulled out from a side road and driven between us and the van. I felt my butterflying stomach lurch as Henry accelerated and drew very close behind the van.

'Can't you flash your lights or hoot or something, Henry?'

'I don't think that would stop them. No, it seems more like they are trying to lose us.'

'What a lark!' Sir Peregrine said, 'Always longed to be in a car chase, what.' He roared with laughter and then added in a more serious voice, 'How's the old battery keeping up, what? Have you got enough juice?'

'Good point, sir, so far so good, but we have under thirty miles, I'd say.'

'Ah well, would be same as if you had an empty tank of petrol, what's that? Nothing to be done.'

I tried the last call number again but it was still on voice mail and so I sat back thinking Sir Perry was right on the ball. Thirty miles seemed a long way but was it long enough?

'Surely they'll swing along to Battersea and cross back over…' I began to say, but at that moment the van took the A2 and my heart joined the butterfly dance as I saw the sign to Dover. 'Oh my God, do you think…'

'I think,' Henry said, 'If I can't stop them soon we shall lose them after thirty miles or so, way before they reach the Channel.'

Sir Peregrine still seemed to be enjoying himself and clapped his hands together as he said, 'What a lark, what? Can't think why anyone would want to get away with a load of old junk, what's that. I mean, maybe the paintings but the old clothes… that scruffy old magic lantern… as for taking it to France… I mean to say, what would the Frogs want with the old junk? Defies all common sense, what?'

I leaned forward again and spoke into Sir Peregrine's ear.

'But you see, Sir Peregrine, if the clothes did belong to Nelson then there are private collectors out there, fanatics… who would pay anything for the great-coat and hat. If Nelson wore them at the Battle of the Nile… well…' I staggered to a halt as I tried to explain the priceless value, and then added feebly, 'Of course, the clothes should be in a museum not in the possession of a greedy collector.'

My last words made Sir Peregrine laugh again as he said,

'Quite right, young Ponsonby, quite right indeed. Greed is a mortal sin, what's that. My Grandpops was one such, I do believe, what. My Mama always said he ruined the family wealth buying for his Horatio collection. He was what you call a greedy fanatic… took things too far, what?'

I exchanged a quick glance with Henry in the driving mirror but we said nothing for a moment. The van was now speeding along the outside lane on the A2 and the traffic had cleared a little. Henry was keeping close enough behind the van to avoid anyone pulling out and getting between us. I looked anxiously at the battery counter and saw it was still showing a green light but if Henry thought we had thirty miles, and if the van was heading to cross the Channel, we would never make it. Then, in the distance ahead I saw the flashing lights of a police car and the traffic began to slow down. The van swerved into the middle lane and Henry just managed to follow, causing two motorists to angrily sound their horns. Now, the van swerved dangerously onto the inside lane and once again Henry followed, causing more road rage.

'He's going to pull off at the next exit.' Henry said, 'I shall get them yet.'

Without indicating, the van did exactly as Henry said and turned violently into the exit marked Gravesend. Henry was even closer behind them now and I found I was holding my breath and clutching Rosso's head.

'But how can you stop them, Henry?' I said, my voice squeaking with fear.

Before Henry could answer the problem was solved. The van driver had underestimated the curve at the end of the exit road and slammed into the barrier and slewed to a halt.

Chapter 40

"He felt like a man who, chasing rainbows, has had one of them suddenly turn and bite him in the leg."

P.G.Wodehouse

'Stay right here, both of you.' Henry said in a hard voice that I hardly recognised. Before I could answer he was out of the car and Rosso had sprung up from the floor in the back and leapt out. I shouted,'

'Henry, don't, they'll have guns, Henry.' But Henry slammed the door and flicked the locks. I scrabbled to open my own door but couldn't open it. I screamed with rage and Sir Peregrine said,

'Stay put, Ponsonby, do as he tells you. What, you'll be safe here.'

To my amazement, he then swung his door open and began to get out. I threw myself over and into the front of the car and pushed past Sir Peregrine and ran toward the van. Henry had already reached the driver's door and just for a moment he glanced back and saw me. I ran forward and went to the rear of the van and Rosso joined me. I tried to open the rear door with some crazy idea that I could pull out the Gainsborough box and the suitcase of clothes. Of course, the van doors were locked tight. Then Henry called out,

'Both men are out for the count. Hurry, Allie, try the door again. I've demobilised the security lock.'

I scrabbled for the inset handle and then Sir Peregrine was beside me and he pushed my hands away and wrenched the doors open wide. We both stood back for a moment and then I saw the suitcase and box neatly tied with webbing to the inside wall of the van. Sir Peregrine said,

'Up you go then, young Ponsonby!'

To my surprise he grabbed me around the waist and hoisted me up and into the van as Rosso sprang in beside me. I pulled at the buckle on the webbing and found it slid open easily and first the box and then the suitcase were soon lying side by side on the van floor. I slid them across to Sir Peregrine who grabbed the suitcase and made off with it to the Alfa at remarkable speed in his old slippers. Before I had managed to jump down, he was back and I pushed the box toward him. His long arms reached out and once again he took hold of it and staggered off to the Alfa. Rosso and I jumped down and I peered cautiously around the back door that was still swinging wide open. Henry immediately saw me and shouted,

'Back to the car, Allie. Back to the car, go, go!'

I noticed he was holding his hand against his hip and I thought he might be hurt but I ran for it, expecting a hail of bullets to follow me but everything was quite eerily silent. No traffic passed in either direction and I jumped into the back of the Alfa and slammed the door closed. Rossi had gone around the van to meet Henry but now I saw them both legging it full tilt back to the Alfa. Rosso leapt straight over the driver's seat and landed on my lap and Henry threw himself into the driving seat and pulled away before he had even shut his door.

We all sat in silence for a moment and then Sir Peregrine said,

'Getting away before the rozzers turn up, what?'

Henry suddenly laughed and turned half around to me and said,

'You and Sir Perry should take up crime. I thought I asked you to stay in the car?'

'Eyes on the road, please Henry. You are our designated getaway driver, so drive.'

'Certainly, Madam!' Henry nodded and accelerated around a roundabout, dramatically skidding the back wheels.

Sir Peregrine slapped his knee and said, 'What a lark, eh? We've got the booty in the boot, what's that? Were the chaps in the van dead, then?'

'No, just a bit dazed.' Henry said, his usual casual voice returning, 'There will be a lot of explaining to do when the police turn up. I thought it best to get away.'

'Quite right, quite right, young man, least said soonest mended and all that, what?'

'But, but… surely we can't just drive off?' Even to my own ears my question sounded pathetic.

'But, but…' Henry mimicked my voice making it sound even more girlish, 'But, but we just did. Hadn't you better call your friend at the V & A. We're running awfully late.'

I stared out of the window for a moment and idly stroked Rosso while I tried to work out a reasonable objection. Rosso pressed his long head onto my knee and sighed. I felt a ridiculous urge to giggle and then found I couldn't stop it and I laughed out loud.

'Feeling better, my love?' Henry said, glancing at me in the driving mirror. His dark eyebrows were raised in the way I loved most and I nodded and tried to stop laughing as I pulled out my mobile.

'Hello, Marianne?' I took a deep breath and tried for a serious voice, 'Sorry, we're running late. What time do you finish work?'

'Oh, don't worry, I'll be here until very late. I'm working on this marvellous tapestry and I want to get it finished for an exhibition. Securicor phoned to say they had called at Coutts but the collection was cancelled or something so I guessed you were held up.'

'Yes, you could say there was a hold up.' I had put my phone on loudspeaker and there was a splutter of laughter from Sir Peregrine at my choice of words. I carried on, 'There's a lot of traffic, quite a jam, in fact, but if you're sure you don't mind we should be with you in less than an hour.'

'That's fine darling, but come around to the staff entrance, I'll tell the gateman to expect your car. So, do you have the artefacts with you then? What happened to Securicor?'

'Well, Securicor turned out not to be quite as secure as we expected, so we have everything in the boot of Henry's car. It's an old dark green Alfa.'

'Fine, I'll tell Jim to expect then. Obviously our security is very tight so just call me again when you get nearby. Can't wait to see you, Allie. Bye.'

'Bye, Marianne and thanks so much.'

I slipped my phone back in my bag and leant my head back against the headrest and closed my eyes. It all seemed ridiculously easy now.

Chapter 41

"It is a good rule in life never to apologise. The right sort of people do not want apologies, and the wrong sort take a mean advantage of them."
                                            P.G.Wodehouse

'I just can't believe it!' My friend, Marianne was holding her hands up to her flushed pink cheeks and almost squeaking. I had known her since Uni days and never had I seen her so excited and flustered. She was normally a Mona Lisa type, all secret smiles and inner calm. Now she turned away from the Gainsborough light-box and looked wildly around her studio.

'Candles, we need candles to light the back. I refuse to let you use electricity.'

She began to delve into a long drawer under her work bench and pulled out three long candles, then held them up and added, 'Matches?'

Henry quickly pulled out his lighter and I was surprised to see that he had refilled it. When and how had he done that? It seemed such a short time since it had run out on us in the attic… and yet it seemed an age. Marianne pushed the lighted candles into a silver candelabra which stood amongst other silverware on the bench behind her.

'Perfect.' She said, her voice now just a whisper and I noticed her hand shaking as she held the candelabra and carried it to a third bench at right angles to the others. She turned to us and said, 'You see, the candlelight is diffused through the silk and… I'll explain later.' She said hurriedly, 'Sir Peregrine you should have first look.'

Sir Peregrine ambled forward toward the hooded visor at the top of the box then said, 'No, no, the honour is all yours, m'dear young lady, what. You're the expert and we are all most terribly obliged to you, what's that.'

I was impressed with the polite and rather stately way he spoke although he then spoiled it a little by adding, with a small snorting laugh,

'Besides, seen them all before, don't you know, just a few pretty landscapes as I recall, nothing to write home about, what?'

Marianne blinked rapidly and then, as though she could wait no longer she quickly pressed her forehead against the box. There was a device of some sort on the side of the box that she turned to move the slides across. I saw her shoulders quivering as she stood looking into the box and saying nothing. I was impatient, too, and said,

'So, Marianne, what can you see?'

She made no reply for a moment and then finally stood up very straight and said very calmly, 'There is no doubt in my mind that these are works by Gainsborough, in fact, the glass slides are in even better condition than the ones we hold here in the museum. Take a look, Allie.'

I moved forward quickly to take my turn and as the first slide moved behind the small silk screen I saw a vivid green landscape flickering with the candlelight behind. The trees seemed to move with a gentle wind against a pale blue Suffolk sky and the river shimmered with silvery luminescence. I cranked the small knob on the side and another view clicked into place. Now, it was a rustic scene of three cows in a grassy pasture and a young boy with a stick. The flickering light gave the illusion of cows moving slowly across the dewy grass. There were ten more scenes, all enchanting in their simplicity and the last, a moonlit scene simply took my breath away. I stood up and turned around and said huskily,

'They're magical, look Henry, each one is perfect.'

Henry took my place and I heard him give a small sigh of pleasure as the first slide moved back into place.

'Sir Peregrine,' I said, 'The paintings are so beautiful.'

'Jolly good, young Ponsonby, I'm sure you know your stuff and this clever young lady, too. I'll be delighted if the museum wants them, of course, what?'

There was an awkward silence and before Marianne could reply, Henry turned away from the light-box and said,

'Well, Sir Peregrine, there should be a valuation first, of course. Don't forget you need some funds to repair your roof. I expect the Victoria and Albert will be interested in bidding if the light-box went to auction.'

There was another even more awkward silence until Sir Peregrine said,

'Expect you're right, old chap, but we can see later, what's that? How about opening up the suitcase of Nelson's clobber next, eh, what?'

Henry lifted the suitcase onto the bench and, again, I noticed he held one hand against his hip. I looked at him anxiously but he seemed only interested in opening the catches on the suitcase and I decided it was not the moment to ask him if he was hurt.

Marianne gave a little gasp as Henry carefully pulled out the great-coat and then the bicorne hat. She laid her hand lightly on one of the lapels and said excitedly,

'The cloth is right for the age, Battle of the Nile, you say, 1798 then.' She took the hat in her hand and held it under an angle-poise lamp and added, 'Of course, Greenwich would want to see this. I have a friend working there and he restored Nelson's Trafalgar coat. Wonderful work... finding blood stains and the bullet hole in the left shoulder... hmm, a bullet from the French sharpshooter that finished him off. In fact, it's one of the most poplar items at the National Maritime Museum... history brought to life, so to speak. It's a splendid vice-admiral's undress coat in fine blue wool... very like this one, I'd say.'

As she spoke, Marianne was very carefully spreading out the great-coat on a white sheet. Her voice was dreamy now as she carried on,

'Hmm, a stand-up collar, button-back lapels and wonderful gold trimmings in remarkably good condition.' Then her voice went squeaky again and she said, 'Oh my God, look, there's a small loop on the right sleeve to hook it up to a lapel button.' She turned to look at us all, her eyes stretched wide. 'Of course, he had lost his right arm the year before at the Battle of Santa Cruz de Tenerife in 1797....' Another moment of silence and then Henry said quite casually,

'I read somewhere that the Maritime Museum suffered from a serious theft in 1951... the Chelengk diamond brooch that Sultan Selim of Turkey presented to Nelson after the success of the Battle of the Nile.'

'It's true,' Marianne said, 'Stolen and never recovered. A disaster for the Museum and for history. It was thought to have been stolen by a criminal gang and broken up and sold on. So many valuable diamonds and an intricate piece of jewellery lost forever.'

Henry reached into his hip pocket and placed a small velvet bag on the table and said quietly,

'Or perhaps not, what's that?'

Epilogue   Christmas Eve

It was Christmas Eve and, as we stopped outside my parent's front door, I looked up at the sky which had that heavy laden look of pending snow.

'I do believe we may have a white Christmas, Henry, look at the sky.'

Henry peered up through the windscreen and said, 'Hmm, high stratus clouds do often mean a snowfall.'

'A white Christmas would be perfect as long as everyone gets here first.' I said, ignoring Henry's cleverness and then added happily,'I believe every Christmas should be white.'

'I suppose you believe in Father Christmas coming down the chimney with your presents, too?'

'Why, of course, I do. Ma and Pa were so good at stockings. Sam and I used to pretend to be asleep and then as soon as they had hung the filled stockings on our beds and gone off to their own room we used to get up and open everything.'

'Weren't you supposed to wait until Christmas morning?'

'Why, of course, but we would stuff everything back and pretend to be surprised and delighted as we reopened it all.'

Henry laughed and said, 'It must have been such fun to have Sam as your brother.'

I felt a pang of guilt as I realised how lonely little Enrico must have been, especially at Christmas time. I said quickly,

'Well, this Christmas, white or not, is going to be very jolly.'

We stepped out of the car and Rosso leapt out and made a grand dash around the rose garden and was soon joined by two Labradors.

'Looks as though Florrie and Sir Peregrine are already here,' Henry said as he began to unload the boot, 'It was very good of your mother to invite them.'

'Oh, she loves a full house. She told me that Florrie only agreed to come if she could help Ma in any way.'

'Not with the cooking, I hope,' Henry laughed, 'Your mother is such a fine cook.'

'Don't worry, Ma would never let anyone take over cooking but we are all allowed to wash up.'

'Quite right,' said Henry, 'I wonder if Mamma and Federico have arrived yet?'

'I doubt it. Your Mamma likes to make a Contessa-style late entrance as far as I recall. Maybe Sam and Suzie are here though.'

As though hearing his name, Sam came out of the front door and held out his arms wide in greeting.

'Merry Christmas to both of you. Did you have a good journey?'

Sam gave me a bear hug and then shook hands with Henry. 'Come on in, it's cold but that sort of quiet cold that means snow… do you think we'll have a white Christmas?'

'Your sister hopes so,' said Henry as he hefted his usual large Louis Vuitton bag out of the boot and threw my back pack over one shoulder, 'she's been like an excited kid all the way down here.'

'Suzie's just the same, it must be a girl thing, I suppose.'

I gave Sam a punch in his abdomen and said, 'Where is Suzie?'

'She's in the kitchen under Ma's supervision messing around with icing sugar and mince pies. I was banned as I dared to eat one before it was decorated or something.'

We made our way into the hall and Henry stopped under the central chandelier that was festooned with red ribbons and a large bunch of mistletoe. He put down our luggage and held out his arms.'

'Isn't this one of the best Christmas traditions, Allie, kiss me Hardy?'

I went over to him and gave him a long hard kiss.

'I've had quite enough of Horatio Nelson for a while now.' I said and kissed him again.

There was a voice from behind me and my father roared out,

'All rubbish, Nelson's dying words were Kismet. He knew Trafalgar was his fate.'

'No, Pa, the word Kismet wasn't in general parlance at the time. No, much more likely he said 'Kiss my Emma, Hardy.' I'm sure of it.' I turned around, still under the mistletoe and looked at my father who laughed aloud and said,

'Always the sharpest knife in the box, Alicia. Little know-all! Now, do I get a Christmas kiss from my favourite daughter?'

He held his arms wide and I ran into them and kissed his cheek as he spun me around. Then, as he set me back down on the flagstones, I said severely,

'You, Pa, have a lot to answer for…sending us off to the perils of Farley Hall.'

'Perry's been telling me all about it but I'm damned if I understood all of it. However, I did gather he's donated Nelson's great-coat and hat to the V &A.'

Henry and I nodded and then the dogs ran in through the front door and our family dog emerged from the kitchen door and joined in as they circled around us barking madly.

Sam and my father chased them into the boot room and then we all made our way into the kitchen.

'There you are!' My mother swept towards us a in a flurry of flour and icing sugar and kissed us both. 'Merry Christmas to you both. How lovely you both look… are you freezing? Florrie and Perry are in the breakfast room by the fire and Suzie has just gone through, too. I'll grab a tray of mince pies and I think we should all join them.' She glanced out of the long window at the end of the kitchen and said, 'Looks like snow to me. How wonderful!'

Henry and I followed the others and I whispered in Henry's ear,

'I hope Sir Peregrine hasn't told them too much… not all the dangerous bits.'

Henry nodded, 'Your father would never forgive me for letting you climb down that roof. I can't forgive myself.'

He shuddered and I nudged him in the ribs as we entered the breakfast room. Sir Peregrine had been sitting in an armchair by the window but as soon as he saw me he jumped up and said,

'There you are, young Ponsonby, slid down any icy roofs lately, what?'

His words were lost in the general hubbub of greetings but I saw Sam look at me sharply and raise his eyebrows. Then, Suzie came over to me and kissed me on both cheeks,

'Als, Merry Christmas, Sir Peregrine has just been telling us about your latest finds. We want to hear all about it.'

There was a moment of silence in the room, partly because everyone was eating a mince pie and I said,

'Oh, you don't want to hear about it... maybe later.'

'No, no, no,' Sam shook his head and frowned at me, 'Sir Peregrine has been saying that we had to hear it all from you and then dropping little hints. No excuse, Sis, we want to hear all about it.'

'Well,' I said reluctantly, 'If you insist but it's a long story so I think I'll start at the end. You see, the final triumph was that Henry had found Nelson's diamond brooch and it's worth millions and millions. Henry, you tell them. I want one of Ma's mince pies. I'm famished.'

'I've never understood how your daughter can be such a skinny little thing and yet she's always eating like a horse.' Henry said, which earned him another, sharper dig in the ribs from my elbow.

'Ouch, I felt that,' said Sam, 'Allie has the sharpest elbows on the planet and she's a Miss Piggy.'

I glared at Sam and said,

'So, you don't want to hear about Nelson's relics, then?'

My father came over to me and put his arm around my shoulders,

'Don't let those boys bully you, my darling, and I for one am longing to know about Nelson.'

'Well, just for you then, Pa, I'll continue although it's Henry's story, really. He found a trunk in one of the attics at Farley Hall and recognised that among the dressing-up clothes there was this amazing great-coat and bicorne hat. He also found, although he sneakily didn't let on at the time, the diamond brooch, known as the Chelengk, the very one that the Sultan of Turkey presented to Nelson after the Battle of the Nile.'

'Good God,' my father said looking shocked, 'But it was stolen years ago and never found.'

Sir Peregrine, holding aloft a mince pie in one hand said,

'To think I played with it when I was a boy, don't you know. Jasper and I used to lark around up there with all the junk. Never knew the old brooch was diamonds, what's that.'

'It's the most intricate piece of jewellery,' said Henry, 'Fortunately, you didn't break it. It's quite delicate and has thirteen sprays of diamonds representing each of the French ships destroyed or captured at the battle. As if that was not enough, the huge central star diamond turns by clockwork. Quite extraordinary craftsmanship. Until 1951 it was the prize of the Maritime Museum.'

Sir Peregrine gave a sudden guffaw of laughter,

'Until my grandfather had it stolen, what's that. Paid a fortune to some villains to nab it for him.'

Now everyone was looking at Sir Peregrine in astonishment and Florrie spoke up quietly,

'That's why, dear heart, we've decided to give it back, haven't we? No good comes from stealing, now does it?'

Henry and I exchanged glances as this was news to us.

Henry began, 'But Florrie, it's an immensely valuable…'

Florrie interrupted in the same quiet voice,

'A-course it is, mighty valuable and should be for all to see. We haven't had time to tell you yet, that nice young woman at the Victoria and Albert museum is donating the coat and that old hat to the Greenwich place, too. What a fine exhibit that'll be when's all tidied up.'

Sir Peregrine was nodding happily and eating his mince pie and there was another moment of silence. Then Henry said,

'And you've donated the Gainsborough light-box to the V & A, too, Sir Peregrine?' Henry looked anxious as he added, 'You do still have a large number of Chinese Choppendale chairs and the Hepplewhites but…'

Sir Peregrine nodded, his mouth too full to reply but Florrie interrupted Henry,

'There now, don't you fret, Henry, my dear, we had good news from the National Gallery saying as how the Constable is definitely genuine. That's good, isn't it?'

'Certainly,' Henry said, 'That's amazing news… I'm very glad for you.'

There was another pause and I said nervously,

'So have you decided to sell it, Sir Peregrine?'

Sir Peregrine dabbed his mouth with a napkin and said,

'Good God, young Ponsonby, do you think I'm mad? Of course, I shall sell, what's that. Seem to recall you said the last one sold at Christie's for over twenty-million, what?

I was startled that Sir Peregrine had so accurately remembered my words and relieved that he wanted to sell. Before I could reply he carried on,

'My muddy daub must be worth something, what? And I'll being giving you some commission or finding fee, what? Couldn't have done any of all this without you and your Henry. What a lark we had, what? Anyway, there'll be enough to put the roof back on, eh? Mend that hole you made, young Ponsonby?'

He roared with laughter and held his glass out to the jug of mulled wine that my father was serving. My brother looked at me again, frowning, so I quickly changed the subject.

'What did the National say about the other painting, Sir Peregrine? Is it a Gainsborough?'

Sir Peregrine was too happy glugging wine and seemed to have lost interest in the conversation but Florrie said,

'Yes, they say tis genuine but Perry likes it so he's a-going to keep it a while yet.'

'I see,' I said although I wasn't at all sure that I saw anything clearly. It had been three weeks since we had left the V & A, past seven in the evening and dropped Sir Peregrine in his slippers at his club, Boodles. I had called him the next morning to see if he was all right and he had been in very good form and told me that Locke's were delivering him a pair of shoes that had been made for him some months ago. The concierge at his club had arranged a driver to take him back to Norfolk. He was about to end the call when he had remembered to tell me that he had spoken to his old friend, the deputy commissioner in the Metropolitan police, who had agreed to sort out the business of the crashed van. With a snort of laughter he added that it was the least he could do and that it had all been such a lark. All in all, I realised, everything had been sorted out in an old school tie and aristocratic way and that he was only anxious to get back to Florrie and his Labs. We had heard nothing from him since, apart from arranging to meet him at my parents for Christmas. I took a deep breath,

'So, it's all working out well, then? Any news of Jasper and Lady Agatha?'

Florrie came over to me and said quietly,

'That all working out for the best, too, my dear. I don't want to shock you but my Perry and I have been awaiting a long time to be together and, well, now we are. Jasper is taking over the tulip farm and I hopes as how he gets on with it. Lady Agatha was never happy at Farley, it's a dreadful thing to be married off… like an arranged marriage and that's what it was, for sure.'

I nodded and tried to think of what to say but Florrie patted my hand and said,

'Now, you sit down, my dear, have another mince pie and enjoy being with your family. I'm just going to clear away a few bits and pieces in the kitchen.'

I nodded again and then she bustled off and I saw Sir Peregrine watch her leave.

I moved over to the fire and took a mince pie but before I could eat it the door was flung open and Henry's mother, the Contessa di Palliano swept into the room and announced,

'It's snowing!'

Christmas Day

It was morning and very early. There was that special hush surrounding the house that I knew meant it had snowed heavily. Inside my bedroom, my childhood bedroom, I heard Henry talking quietly to Rosso.

'I knew a dog of your intelligence would soon tire of the Labs, but don't feel bad about it Rosso. You can't help being a superhuman dog.'

I stifled a giggle as I wanted to hear how the one-sided conversation carried on. In fact, it wasn't altogether one-sided as Rosso made appropriate sighs and yawn and the occasional snuffling sound. Henry continued,

'And I know you're thinking that you didn't make any outstanding actions in this last adventure but, believe me, Allie and I could not do without you and you'll love our next trip to Verona.'

There was another snuffle and I heard Rosso licking Henry's hand in appreciation. I squeezed my eyes tight shut, as I could feel a gurgle of laughter rising inside me as Henry carried on,

'Nor should you feel jealous of Allie, you don't, do you? I mean she is everything to me but nothing has changed between you and me, has it? Don't forget, either, that sometimes I feel a little jealous myself when you seem to go to her side.'

Rosso gave a loud yawn and came over to the bed and nudged my shoulder. I pretended to wake up and said,

'Morning, Rosso, have you been out already? Your nose is so, so cold.'

'Ah, you're awake at last, my love.' Henry said, coming over to the bed and sitting beside me. 'We've been waiting ages, Merry Christmas!'

I sat up quickly and bounced up and down,

'Oh, I'd forgotten, how could I forget? I've been looking forward to this day for so long. Well, ever since last Christmas Day, really. It's my very favourite day of the year.' I stretched out and patted Rosso and then threw my arms around Henry, 'Happy Christmas, Henry. Has it snowed all night?'

'Yep, and it's still snowing now, shall I open the curtains?'

'No, I'll do it.' I jumped out of bed and ran to the window and peeped out.

'Henry,' I said, turning around, 'Is it very early?'

'Hmm, well, yes, I suppose so… nearly seven, I think.'

I stretched and yawned at the same time and climbed back into the bed, 'Henry, that is very early especially as we went to bed at midnight and then… well, we didn't sleep much, did we?' I pulled the quilt around me and then noticed something weighing it down at the end. I almost screamed and then squeaked, 'There's a stocking on the bed.'

'Really?' Henry said in his best drawling Etonian voice, 'How extraordinary. How did that get there? Fancy Santa Claus managing to drop it off in this weather.'

I gave Henry a gentle push and then threw myself down the bed and grabbed the red felt stocking which jingled most satisfactorily as I held it up.

'It has my name on it, too! It's so posh, it must be Fortnum's. Oh no,' I suddenly pulled a face, 'Santa hasn't left anything for you, Henry or you, Rosso.'

Rosso yawned again and went back to lie beside the long radiator under the window. Henry laughed,

'I think Santa knows that stockings are more of a girl thing. Anyway, you could always share.'

'Hmm, I suppose I could but… let me see.' I untied the green ribbon at the top of the stocking and pulled out a gold tin of chocolate truffles. 'Oh, look, Henry, it is Fortnum's, my favourite chocs. I suppose you'd like one?' I opened the tin and held it out to Henry but he shook his head,'

'Before breakfast? No thanks.'

'Well, I'll eat your share then, dear Henry, you can be so Italian at times. Of course you eat chocolate before breakfast on Christmas Day.'

I put a large truffle into my mouth and closed my eyes in ecstasy.'

'Goodness, you are such a little piggy, Allie, and I've seen that look on your face before… not when you're eating chocolate though.'

'You're scandalous, Enrico di Palliano. Now, next… hmm, this is interesting.' I tore open the tissue paper wrapping and a silk nightdress slid into my hands. I held it up by the thin shoestring straps and admired the midnight blue silk and lace. 'Oh gosh, it's so lovely, I mean, I usually wear pyjamas if I wear anything at all. This is so sophisticated.' I stood up on the bed and slipped it over my head, shivering slightly as the soft silk shimmied down the length of my body.

'Beautiful, my love,' said Henry, 'and how clever of Santa. I think it really counts as a present for me.'

'True,' I nodded in agreement and you mustn't be greedy so all the rest must be mine. Look, here's a neat little package. ' I pulled open the next parcel and found a small silver tape measure. 'Gosh, look Henry, it's so neat. I'm always wanting to measure things up. Thank you.'

'Whatever do you mean? It's Santa you have to thank, not me.'

'True again and there's another little parcel in the same wrapping. Oh, look, a miniature torch. Now, that could come in very useful. I think Santa knows we were stuck in that dark old attic.'

'Don't remind me, please. I saw your father out on my walk this morning and he asked me how it had gone at Farley Hall and whether there had been any problems. He sounded rather suspicious. I know you told me not to say a word about the roof incident or the van hijacking but, honestly, Allie, it was rather difficult.'

'I'm sure you worked the Palliano magic and came up with something, my love.'

'Well, all I could do was to dramatically change the subject.'

'Pa always goes out before the dawn has even cracked to check on the horses. Did you talk about horses then?'

'Er, no, not really but I asked him an important question… but I'll tell you later. Come on, open the next one… only two more.'

'Right, then this one.' I pulled out a square box neatly tied with a wide red ribbon and shook it, 'Either a miniature bottle of brandy or some-such or… I ripped off the gold paper and added, 'Perfume! It's one I've never heard of… but… but it has my name on it?' I stared at Henry in surprise and then carefully unsealed the crystal glass stopper and breathed in. 'Oh, Henry, it's glorious. It smells a bit like you but more flowery, a little sweeter. I love it!'

Henry laughed, 'You are such a clever clogs, aren't you? Even your pretty nose is clever. I ordered it from the parfumerie I use in Grasse to make my own soaps and colognes. My remit was to make my personal perfume slightly more floral and prettier.'

I stared at Henry, 'You have you own scent?'

'Well, it's kept as a reference number in the Fragonard atelier. I've been using it for years. Very good quality, I find.'

'I'm sure. But have you forgotten that the stocking is from Father Christmas?'

'Ah well. He asked my advice on some things, of course, especially the last one in the toe. Go on, open it.'

'Oh, it will be an orange, I know it will.' I pushed my hand into the toe of the stocking and felt a round velvet shape. I squealed with excitement, 'No, it's not an orange. I pulled it out and held in my hand a bright orange velvet box. I drew in my breath and slowly pressed the gold stud to open it. The lid sprang open and inside, resting on pale gold silk there was a sapphire ring. I looked up at Henry, my eyes wide and he took the box from me and slipped the ring into the palm of his hand.

'Allie, Will you marry me?'

I nodded, too surprised to speak and held out my left hand. Henry kissed my hand and said,

'I asked your father earlier, that was the question, of course. He seemed very pleased so, Allie, will you please marry me… and Rosso?'

Rosso heard his name and leapt up from his place by the radiator and bounded onto the bed. Then, we were all bouncing up and down as I said,

'Yes, oh yes, yes, definitely, yes please!'

The End

All my books can be sampled and bought with a click from Amazon or my website:
www.katefitzroy.co.uk

FINE CRIMES

GILT 1: Napoleon's desk on the Riviera

DEAD COPY 2: Rome - Poetic Justice in Jeopardy

DARK MIRROR 3: Loire Valley Marie Antoinette's Trinkets

FAKE 4 Adriatic Riviera Only danger is real

RELIC 5 Norfolk Aristocratic Peril and Christmas

WINE DARK MYSTERIES

Well Chilled Case 1: Haute Savoie to Provence, France

Skin Contact Case 2: Provence, France

Lingering Finish Case 3: Roussillon, France

Rich Earthy Tuscany Case 4: Chianti, Italy

Mistaken Identities Case 5: Frascati, Rome, Italy

Fine Racy Wine Case 6: Newmarket, Suffolk, England

Horizontal Tasting Case 7 Loire Valley, France

Full Bodied Lush Case 8: Gascony, France

Pink Fizz Case 9: Kent, England

Fresh and Fruity Case 10: Verdicchio, Italy

Juicy Ruby Case 11: Bardolino, Italy

Lay Down Case 12: Margaux, France

also…

ROMANTIC THRILLERS

Perfume of Provence

Provence Love Legacy

Provence Flame

Provencal Landscape of Love

Provence Starlight

Provence Snow

Dreams of Tuscany

Moonlight in Tuscany

Love on an Italian Lake

Too Many Men

I hope you enjoy escaping with me and if you have any comments or ideas please email:

fitzroykate@gmail.com

Printed in Great Britain
by Amazon